FROM
THIS
MOMENT

ALSO BY LAUREN BARNHOLDT

FROM THIS MOMENT

THE MOMENT OF TRUTH BOOK 3

LAUREN BARNHOLDT

An Imprint of HarperCollinsPublishers

HarperTeen is an imprint of HarperCollins Publishers.

From This Moment
Copyright © 2015 by Lauren Barnholdt
All rights reserved. Printed in the United States of America.
No part of this book may be used or reproduced in any manner whatsoever without written permission except in the case of brief quotations embodied in critical
articles and reviews. For information address HarperCollins Children's Books, a
division of HarperCollins Publishers, 195 Broadway, New York, NY 10007.
www.epicreads.com

Library of Congress catalog card number: 2014959382
ISBN 978-0-06-232143-5 (pbk.)

Typography by Ellice M. Lee
15 16 17 18 19 CG/RRDH 10 9 8 7 6 5 4 3 2 1

First Edition

FOR BRIANNA, THE STRONGEST GIRL I KNOW

ONE

To: Aven Shepard (aven.shepard@brightonhillshigh.edu)

From: Aven Shepard (aven.shepard@brightonhillshigh.edu)

Before graduation, I will . . . *tell the truth.*

I've thought about that email every single day since I sent it. And if I'm being completely honest, it's kind of been the thing that's gotten me through the past four years.

I know that's ridiculous. I mean, how can a stupid email have kept me going for years? An email I sent to *myself.* An email I hadn't even *received* yet. An email that has nothing surprising in it, since, as previously mentioned, I sent it to myself.

But that email has been my own personal reminder— one that lets me know my life won't be like this forever. That at some point I'll be able to stop wondering, to stop walking around with a huge secret, to stop living a gigantic lie. And most importantly, to stop feeling like my heart is being broken every single day.

Of course, it's easy to find comfort in this when you don't actually have to *do* anything about your life being a big lie. Which is what I've been doing for the past four years. But now the day is here. The day the email is going to be delivered to my in-box. It also happens to be the day of our senior trip to Florida, which is actually kind of perfect.

Because it means I'll have no choice. I'm going to be with Liam all weekend. Which means there won't be any excuse not to tell him the truth—that I've been in love with him ever since we met four years ago.

"Did you bring enough bathing suits?" Izzy asks me. "Because we're going to be in the ocean a lot. And you have to rinse them out every time you wear them. You can't just let your bathing suit sit around in salt water—it wrecks the fabric."

We're standing outside the school, waiting for the bus to show up and take us to the airport, where we're going to board our flight to Siesta Key, Florida. It's an unseasonably cold morning, and I shiver. "I brought three bathing suits," I say. "That should be enough."

"It should be," Izzy agrees. "We just have to make sure we rinse them out as soon as we get back to our room." Izzy is very practical. She's the type who always knows the right thing to do, like last year when Roman Wright almost sliced off his finger using the buzz saw in technology. Everyone else started freaking out and screaming, but Izzy just grabbed a towel out of the back storage closet, wrapped up Roman's bleeding finger, and walked him to the nurse.

Later she told me that afterward she felt faint and had to crouch down in the hallway with her head between her legs until she felt better. But when it was actually happening, she was as calm as could be.

"Yeah," I say. I hop back and forth nervously from one foot to the next and glance down at my phone. That email should be here any minute. At least, I'm hoping it will be.

Lyla, Quinn, and I scheduled them to be sent today. The date has been etched into my brain ever since I hit the send button. I thought it might show up at midnight, but it didn't. I don't think we scheduled them for a specific time. Actually, I know we didn't.

Because I would have remembered that.

It's the most important email I've ever sent in my life.

"Are you okay?" Izzy asks. "You keep checking your phone."

"Oh, yeah, I'm fine," I lie. "Just checking to make sure we didn't miss the bus."

"Why would we have missed the bus?" Izzy asks. "We're early."

It's true. We are early. In fact, we were almost the first

ones here. Izzy likes to get places early, and I kind of go along with it. Although today I was actually glad for her punctuality. I *wanted* to get here early. I want to get this trip going.

It's the trip that's going to change my life, after all.

Good or bad, after today, things will never be the same.

"Oh, I know we haven't missed the bus," I say. "I just meant, like, if they sent out a group text or something. You know, the school. To let us know if the bus is coming."

Izzy frowns at me. "Since when does our school send texts?"

"Since they implemented an emergency alert system," I say. I know because I'm on the Student Action Committee. A lot of people think the Student Action Committee is a joke, and if I'm being completely honest, it kind of is. Its main function is to have an official-sounding name so the administration can pretend the students have a say in their own education. Which is a total joke. We have no power. So even though kids come to us with problems, we can't really do anything about it, because anything we want to do has to be approved by the administration.

The whole thing is totally pointless. But whatever.

I like being on the SAC, because it gives me an extracurricular that has nothing to do with sports, which I'm horrible at, and it's not like yearbook or working on the school website, where you have to do actual work. The Student Action Committee ends up sitting around the library reading gossip magazines while some of us take turns sneaking into the bathroom to share a joint. I don't, of course. Drugs aren't my thing.

"Still," Izzy says. She reaches down and fiddles with the tag on her carry-on bag. The armful of Alex and Ani bracelets she's wearing jangle on her wrist. "This isn't exactly an emergency."

"True."

"Aven, are you okay?" she asks, her blue eyes filled with concern. "You've been acting really weird all morning."

"I'm fine!" I exclaim, realizing I sound kind of frantic. Which is strange, because I feel surprisingly calm for someone who might be about to ruin her entire life. But I can't tell Izzy what's going on. She doesn't know I'm in love with Liam. No one does. Except for me. Well, and Lyla and Quinn. But I'm not friends with them anymore, so they don't count.

"Okay." Izzy pushes her bangs out of her face. They're in that in-between stage, the stage where they're too long to really be bangs, but too short to blend in with her layers or pull back into a ponytail. She frowns and looks like she's going to say something else, but then she looks up across the parking lot and her face breaks into a smile. "Oh!" she says happily. "Here comes Liam!"

I look up.

There he is.

Liam.

My best friend.

The boy I've been in love with for four years.

He walks easily across the parking lot, his black backpack slung over his shoulder, his hair slightly messy, a coffee in one hand. He looks up and spots me and Izzy standing there, and he gives us a wave.

I marvel at how easy he's walking, as if he doesn't have a care in the world. That's always been so strange to me—how one person can have been my whole entire world for the past four years, how his every action, his every word has affected me on such a profound level. The things he's said can either knock me into the stratosphere of happiness, or throw me into the depths of despair.

How can he not know how I feel? How is it that I've been so good at hiding the thing that's been the biggest part of my life for all these years?

"Hey," he says when he sees us. "How are my two favorite girls?"

"Good," I say.

"Great," Izzy says.

She smiles up at him as he leans down and gives her a kiss.

Which is another huge reason that after this weekend nothing will ever be the same. Because after this weekend, my best friend is going to know I'm in love with her boyfriend.

* * *

I'm not a horrible person, I swear.

I never, *ever* meant it to be this way.

And yeah, I know everyone who does something horrible says that exact same thing, but in my case, it's true. It's not like Izzy started dating Liam and then all of a sudden I decided I liked him and we had some torrid affair behind her back.

I saw him first.

And I know that sounds childish, but it's true.

Liam and I have been friends since eighth grade. I'd like to say that back then he was skinny and short and had acne, but it's not true. In fact, he was already on his way to being the six feet tall he is now, and his skin was smooth and perfect except for a few freckles around his nose, which did nothing except give his sexiness a tiny bit of adorable.

We met in health class, which was a totally embarrassing class, because not only did we have to learn about the human body (which is weird when you're with a bunch of eighth-grade boys, and also, let's face it, a little late), we learned how to put condoms on. And not even on a banana either—on this weird fake thing that I guess was supposed to look like a curved plastic penis.

Health was only for half the year, and so the classes tended to be smaller. There were only fourteen people in the class, and all the other girls were from the popular crowd. They all had boobs and hair extensions, and I still had my braces on. None of them even blinked when our teacher, Mrs. Squire, pulled out the condom to show us how to use it.

Anyway, the whole class was just really bizarre, and I couldn't wait for it to be over. But then, for one of our projects, we were given the task of taking care of a fake baby. We all got fake jobs with fake salaries, and we had to come up with a family budget and also make sure to keep these electronic dolls alive. The dolls were creepy, because they had fixed blank stares that made them look like they might come to life at any moment and kill you.

They'd emit these high-pitched screams every so often, and then you'd have to feed them a bottle, or change them, or play with them. Of course, the whole exercise was supposed to show us that being in charge of a baby was extremely difficult, and so we should make sure to use those condoms they'd told us about. Our grade was going to be based on how well we took care of the baby—the stupid thing had a computer in its back that would keep track of how quickly you responded to its wailing. The faster you responded, the better your grade would be.

Of course, no one else in the class really cared about their health grade. Health was considered a bullshit class, one that no one wanted to put any effort into. The boys decided to make a contest out of who could kill the baby the fastest. (Of course, the baby couldn't actually die, because it was a doll. But still, if you didn't take care of it, when you opened the back, the computer would flash "ABUSE" "NEGLECT" or "DEAD" in big green letters. It was actually pretty horrible when you think about it. And I felt really bad for our teacher, because she was a first year who had a degree in English but got stuck teaching health because there were no jobs in the English department. The poor woman just wanted to teach us about all the symbolism in *To Kill a Mockingbird*, and instead she ended up trying to make sure we kept our babies alive and knew how to put a condom on a fake penis. And most of us killed our babies, which meant she was one for two.)

Anyway, I remember being really intimidated when I found out I had to have a fake husband, and even more intimidated when I found out it was Liam. Not that I was the type of girl who got all crazy about boys—at least, not the way some girls in my class did. I mean, I had my favorite celebrities and pop stars, but I'd never really had a huge crush on a real-life boy.

Until I met Liam.

He was gorgeous.

And nice.

He didn't try to kill our baby.

He probably wanted to—all his friends were doing it, and

I'm sure he thought it was funny. But he knew my grades were important to me. I wasn't going to fail health just because some popular kids wanted to make a mockery out of the whole thing. So Liam took care of that dumb baby, even when it kept him up until three o'clock in the morning the day before his lacrosse tryouts.

I was in love with him from the second we got our A.

And I've been in love with him ever since.

"I have something for you to listen to," Liam says to us as we're boarding the bus to the airport.

"Oh," I say. "Okay."

Liam's a musician. He makes electronica on one of these weird machines called an Ableton Push. It plays drums and keyboards and guitar, only electronically. I can't figure out how to use it, but I love the music Liam makes, and not just because I'm in love with him. He's super talented.

"You can borrow my headphones," Izzy whispers to me under her breath, and I try not to feel annoyed. I love Izzy, and she's usually really nice. But she doesn't like Liam's music. Actually, that's not totally true. It's not that she doesn't *like* Liam's music, it's that she doesn't really *get* it. It's not like the stuff you hear on the radio. It's more of an underground, niche kind of sound, the sort of thing you have to seek out on YouTube or look up on SoundCloud. But still. Would it kill her to be a little more supportive? I give her a tight smile.

Once we're on the bus, Izzy slides into a seat with Hartley Parsons.

"You don't want to sit in back with us?" I ask.

"Nah," Izzy says, waving her hand. "You guys go ahead and listen to Liam's music."

"Okay," I say. It's not unusual for Liam and me to have time alone without Izzy. Even though the two of them are a couple, they're not, like, inseparable or anything. And Izzy is either really secure, or she doesn't see me as a threat at all, because she doesn't care if Liam and I spend time alone.

Liam picks a seat in the back, then pulls out his iPhone and hands it to me.

"Here," he says, and I stick Izzy's earbuds into my ears.

Liam turns the song on, and I lean my head back against the seat and close my eyes. I like to close my eyes when I listen to music, any music, but especially Liam's songs. I feel like I need to block everything out while I let the beats move over me. Liam's music doesn't have lyrics. It's just the rhythm of the electronica. Every once in a while he'll pull out his acoustic guitar and strum a little bit, but it's always just a melody or something. He doesn't sing.

This new one is good, and I tap my foot along with it.

When it's over, I don't even realize that the bus has pulled out of the school parking lot and is on its way to the airport.

"Liam, it's awesome," I say, handing the phone back to him. "I really like it."

"Thanks," he says. "Do you think it's uploadable?"

He means to his SoundCloud account. "Definitely," I say. "You should upload it immediately."

But he's not listening to me anymore. He's looking down at something in his hand. My phone. I must have handed it to him so I'd have my hands free to take his.

"What's this?" he asks.

"What's what?" I look down at my screen, praying my mom hasn't sent me some kind of humiliating text asking me if I remembered to pack underwear or something.

"You sent an email to yourself." He looks at me guiltily. "Sorry, the notification just popped up on the screen."

I look down at the notification. One new email from Aven Shepard. I know what it says before I even open it.

To: Aven Shepard (aven.shepard@brightonhillshigh.edu)
From: Aven Shepard (aven.shepard@brightonhillshigh.edu)
Before graduation, I will . . . *tell the truth.*

"Oh," I say, trying to keep my voice steady. "That's . . . weird."

"Yeah." He looks at me, his eyes serious, and I wonder again how we can have spent so much time together and he can have no idea how I really feel.

Tell him.

Do it now.

Tell him the email is about him, that you sent it to yourself years ago, that you've been in love with him all this time, that it's driving you crazy, that you need to know if he feels the same way.

I open my mouth, not believing that it's going to happen here, on a random bus ride, before the trip even begins.

"Oh, well," Liam says, giving me back my phone. "It's probably just spam."

"What?"

"Spam. You know, like when your email gets hacked?"

I have no idea what he's talking about.

"It happened to me once before," he says, shrugging. "It's when someone mirrors your email address and makes it seem like you're emailing yourself. You know, for an advertisement or something?"

"Oh," I say, shoving my phone into my bag. "Yeah. Definitely."

"You should change your password," he says.

"I will." Not.

"Hey," he says, looking at me. "You okay?"

"Yeah," I say. "I'm fine." I turn and look out the window, watching the blur of houses and cars going by, blinking fast to stop myself from crying. Why would I even cry? It's not like I told him and he rejected me. At least not yet.

"Aven," Liam says. "What's wrong? Are you worried about your writing?"

"My writing?"

"Yeah, that someone is going to get it from your email?"

"Oh. Um, yeah." I'm working on a novel. I have been for the past six months or so. Liam keeps bugging me to read it, but I haven't let him yet. He thinks it's because I'm some supersecret artist, but the truth it, I can't let him read it because it's kind of about us.

Well, not exactly. It's about a girl who's in love with her best friend. I know it's cheesy, but they always say to write what you know. And that's what I know. The novel started out as a short story I wrote in creative writing, this sort of slice-of-life vignette based on something that happened with me and Liam.

It was all about this girl who was sitting in a car with her best guy friend after a movie. And they're just sitting there, talking about the movie and all kinds of other things, but all the girl can think about is how bad she wants the boy to kiss her. And it's this weird running loop in her head, where everything is completely normal on the outside, but inside she's just freaking out. The whole story takes place over, like, ten minutes, but it feels much longer because of the girl's thoughts.

My teacher loved it—she gave me an A plus and told me it was one of the best-written things she'd read in her five years of teaching the class. She told me I had a great imagination and an aptitude for writing.

I believed her about the aptitude for writing part, since I'd always scored really well in English and on any kind of verbal standardized tests. But the imagination part I wasn't so sure about.

I mean, nothing in the story was really made up—the exact thing had happened to me when Liam had driven me home from a movie the weekend before. It was this twisty sci-fi indie movie that Izzy had refused to see with him, and we talked about the characters and the plot and if the premise really worked, and I sat there the whole time wishing more than anything he would kiss me.

The only thing in the story that had been made up was the ending—in the story, the boy reached over and unhooked the girl's seat belt and kissed her and it was perfect. In real life, Liam had looked at the clock and said it was getting late and he needed to get home so he could call Izzy before he went to bed.

I got out of the car and went inside and threw myself down on my bed and stared at the ceiling for a while, and then I opened a fresh Word document and wrote the story. It made me feel better, like I was rewriting the ending of my life or something.

After that, I started writing more about me and Liam, and somewhere along the way I realized my little stories would make a pretty good book. It's more than halfway written now, and I think when it's done I'm going to try to do something with it, like send it to publishers and see if there's any interest.

"No one's going to steal your writing," Liam says. "I promise. Those hackers are just looking for passwords so they can send out a bunch of phishing emails from your account. If you reset your password, it should be fine."

"Thanks," I say. "Because yeah, it would totally suck if my writing got out there." *Especially to you,* I think. Ha-ha.

By the time the bus pulls into the airport, I'm starting to think listening to that email might not be such a good idea. I know I sent it as a way to set a deadline for myself, to make sure I told Liam how I felt before graduation. But when you really think about it, nothing good can come of it.

I mean, if he says he doesn't feel the same way, I'm going to be upset, and it's going to ruin not only the rest of my trip, but probably the rest of my senior year. If he says he *does* feel the same way, then I'm going to have to figure out a way to tell Izzy.

But the biggest reason not to tell Liam is because I don't like the way all this obsessing is making me feel. My life is about more than Liam. Yes, I like him a lot. Yes, I might be in love with him. Yes, it's hard to see him with someone else and pretend I only like him as a friend, especially when I think he and I are perfect for each other.

But do I really want to spend the whole trip obsessing about him like this? It's ridiculous.

The bus lurches to a stop, and Liam stands up. "You ready?" he asks.

"Yes," I say firmly, grabbing my bag and following him down the aisle.

It's all settled.

Email or not, deadline or not, some secrets are just supposed to stay that way.

T W O

BUT AS WE WALK INTO THE AIRPORT, MY phone starts buzzing.

I look down.

Before graduation, I will . . . *tell the truth.*

Crap. Lyla, Quinn, and I set those dumb emails to repeat all day so that we couldn't ignore them.

Wait.

Lyla, Quinn, and I . . . that means those two are probably going to get their emails today, too! My heart leaps. I'm always looking for an excuse to talk to Lyla and Quinn. They were my best friends until we got into a stupid fight a couple of years ago, and I've never really gotten over it.

"Are you okay?" Liam asks. "You're acting kind of out of it."

"I'm fine!" I say a little too brightly. "I'm just . . . ah, you know, afraid to fly." It's a lie. I'm not afraid of flying. I love to fly. I bring one of those little masks you wear over your eyes and I fall right asleep. I like knowing I'm up in the sky, floating through the clouds and not even really being able to tell unless the plane hits some turbulence . . . it's very soothing, everything being blocked out.

"Since when are you afraid to fly?" Liam asks. "You love flying."

"*Usually* I do," I say. "But, ah, the terror alert level was raised this morning."

He wrinkles his forehead. "No, it wasn't."

"Yeah, I think it was. I saw something about it on Twitter."

"That would be a really big deal," he says. "So I think we would have heard about it." He reaches over and takes my bag from me. He's such a gentleman. Most guys my age wouldn't even notice that I have a bag, and here Liam is, taking it from me so I don't have to carry it. He's so sweet.

"Well, maybe not," I say.

"Maybe we wouldn't have heard about it?"

"No, maybe . . . maybe I got it wrong," I trail off lamely. Wow. I really am acting a little crazy today. I think it's because I'm too in my head. Usually I work my problems out by talking them through with someone. Like Liam. Or Izzy. But obviously I can't talk about this problem with either one of them.

I try to imagine what they would say if I asked them

about it, if I wasn't talking about Liam, if it was some other guy I was in love with. Liam would probably tell me to go for it. He would say, "Any guy who doesn't like you back isn't worth it, Aven" and "You have to take some risks, Aven" and "I can't believe you've been in love with this guy for years and you haven't told him, Aven." It's weird, thinking about Liam giving me advice about some imaginary guy and telling me that if a guy doesn't like me, he's not worth it.

Izzy would tell me to keep my mouth shut. She'd say that if a guy liked me, he'd let me know, that there's no way any teenage boy could go years being friends with a girl and not tell her how he really felt.

"I'm going to go grab a soda before we board," Liam says. "You want anything?"

"No, that's okay."

He leaves, and I take a deep breath and look around the airport. I pick a seat in the middle of the boarding area and sit down. I'm all jittery, though, the calmness I was feeling this morning apparently deciding it was done with me.

A few seconds later, someone taps me on my shoulder, and I'm so keyed up I almost scream.

But it's only Izzy.

"Hi," I say. "Where've you been? We were looking for you when we got off the bus, but we couldn't—"

"Can I talk to you for a second?" she asks, cutting me off. Her eyes look a little wild.

"Oh," I say. "Um, yeah, sure."

She glances around, like she's looking to see if someone's watching us. "Where's Liam?" she asks.

"Oh," I say. "He went to get a soda. Do you want to talk to him, too?"

"No!" Izzy shakes her head vehemently. She grabs my hand and grips it so hard I'm afraid she's going to leave marks. "I can't talk to Liam. I . . . I need to talk to you alone."

"Okay," I say. Wow. She sounds serious. And whatever she has to tell me must have something to do with Liam. Something she doesn't want him to hear. Is she going to break up with him? Is she going to dump him right here in the airport, before we even go on our trip?

Will Liam be upset? Will I have to console him the whole time we're in Florida, stroking his hair and letting him listen to sad music? I'll order him pizza and get beer somehow, letting him eat and drink his sorrows away, until finally we'll fall into bed together, our limbs intertwined, our lips just inches from touching.

"I always thought you were too good for her," I'll whisper.

And then he'll kiss me.

Of course, I don't want to be his rebound. Or his drunken hookup. That would defeat the whole purpose. So maybe we won't hook up that night. My fantasy changes to one of me consoling Liam all night, until he finally feels well enough for a walk on the beach the next morning, the kind of walk that involves a splash fight and him picking me up and twirling me around before setting me down gently on the sand. The kind of walk that ends with Liam pushing my hair off my face while he gazes down at me, his eyes on mine as it hits him in that moment how perfect we are together.

"We can't talk here," Izzy says, pulling me out of my fantasy. "We need to go somewhere private."

I glance around, but there's really nowhere private to go when our whole senior class (minus Stori Knolls and Taylor Racine, who couldn't attend due to disciplinary action against them for a huge scandal that involved shoplifting and filing a false police report) is surrounding us.

"The bathroom," Izzy declares. She practically wrenches my arm out of my socket pulling me toward the restrooms, which are surprisingly deserted.

There's a woman washing her hands at one of the sinks, but that's about it. Still, Izzy insists on looking under every single stall door, making sure no one's there, listening.

"I don't think anyone's in here," I offer helpfully, but she just shoots me a look and continues with her detective work.

Wow. She must really not want anyone to know what it is she's about to tell me. Can it really be that bad? Maybe she cheated on Liam! Maybe she cheated on Liam and now she's going to break up with him so she can be with her new guy.

I'll bet it's John Travers. She's always flirting with him

during lunch, stealing chicken tenders off his plate and pretending she's into the weird heavy metal music he's always listening to. Also, I'm pretty sure she stole some pictures of him from the yearbook office. She had these printouts of him that fell out of her notebook a few weeks ago, which I thought was kind of weird. She's not even on yearbook, but her friend Sarah is, and she probably—

"Come on," Izzy says, pulling me into a stall.

"Okay," I say, shaking my head once we're inside. "This is awkward. Can't we just talk out there?"

"Someone could come in," Izzy says. And that's when I notice her blue eyes are filled with tears. They're even more blue when they're all watery like that. Liam has blue eyes, too. Which means that if the two of them ever had a kid, their child would have blue eyes. I have brown eyes. Which means if *I* had a kid with Liam, it *might* have blue eyes, but most likely it would end up with normal old muddy brown. We learned all about it in tenth-grade biology.

I wonder if that's why Liam's predisposed to be with Izzy instead of me. Maybe it's just simple genetics. Like he needs to be with someone who has blue eyes to keep his genes relevant or something. It's like how girls are attracted to strong guys because they're the ones who will be able to keep the population going. Although I'm not sure how having blue-eyed children is good for evolution. Maybe it's more about protecting what you have.

Quinn would know. Quinn, my ex-best friend, is into all that science-y stuff. She wants to be a doctor, and she's going to Stanford in the fall. At least, that was her plan. I try not to think about the fact that I haven't talked to Quinn in two years, that I have no idea if her college plans have changed, if she even wants to be a doctor anymore.

You'll talk to her this weekend, a little voice in my head whispers. *After what you did with the room assignments, you'll be forced to.*

But I push that thought out of my mind immediately. I should really only be dealing with one friendship issue at a time. Not that Quinn's my friend anymore. But still. I need to deal with Izzy, and the fact that she's standing right here in front of me, looking like maybe she's about to burst into tears.

"Iz," I say. "Sweetie, what's wrong?"

"It's Liam," she says. She takes a deep breath, and I can tell she's trying really hard not to cry. "Aven, you can't tell him what I'm about to tell you." She shakes her head vehemently, like whatever she's about to say is some kind of state secret or something. "I feel awful asking you to keep a secret from him, but I don't know what else to do. I don't have anyone else to talk to about this, and I'm at my wit's end."

"Okay," I say automatically, starting to feel really concerned. I know I was hoping that maybe Izzy cheated on Liam, but that was just a fantasy. I don't want Izzy to be hurting. I don't want her to be this upset.

"I think Liam's cheating on me," she says.

"What?" I shake my head. "Izzy, that's crazy."

"Is it?" she asks. "Is it really?"

"Yeah. Liam would never do that to you." It's true. I'm not just saying that to make her feel better. Liam would never cheat on anyone. He's too good and perfect.

Izzy gives a bitter little laugh, which is actually kind of disturbing. It makes her sound slightly deranged.

"Um, well, why do you think he's cheating on you?" I ask gently.

She reaches into her purse and pulls out a packet of Swedish Fish. She rips open the packet and hands one to me. I reach out and take it, then pop it into my mouth. Izzy always has candy on hand, because she's hypoglycemic. If her blood sugar starts to fall, she needs to eat something sweet right away or she could faint. When I first met her, I found it really annoying, the way she was always pulling candy out and eating it. Everything about her was just so damn *delicate*. At first I even thought she might be lying about it. Or at least exaggerating. And then one night we went to the movies and she almost collapsed on the way out. I had to buy her Sour Patch Kids and an extra-large soda.

"He's just been acting really weird lately." She bites the head off a fish rather aggressively. "He's always on his phone, and he's been making excuses to avoid spending time with me."

"He's been busy," I say. "With his music."

"No one's that busy with their music," she says. "And besides, since when does his music get in the way of hanging out?"

She's right. Even when Liam would be super into making his songs, he'd always do it late at night, or invite Izzy and me over to keep him company while he worked. We'd sit and watch movies in his basement and eat snacks while he composed songs on the computer. He'd play them for us when he was done and ask our opinions, and Izzy would roll her eyes while I gave him my feedback.

But Izzy's right. We haven't been doing that lately. I just figured maybe Izzy and Liam were finally getting sick of me being the third wheel all the time and had started hanging out alone.

"Just because Liam wants to make music by himself doesn't mean he's cheating on you," I say. "He probably just wants to be alone. Maybe he got sick of us bothering him." It could definitely be true. Sometimes if Izzy and I get bored, our behavior starts devolving. One time we started having giggling fits and throwing gummy worms at the back of Liam's head. It was extremely childish. Not that he really seemed to mind that much. But maybe he was just being nice.

"It's not just that," she says. "It's . . . we haven't had sex in a couple of weeks."

"Oh." My face burns. Of course I knew they were having sex. At least, I assumed they were. Why wouldn't they be? They've been together for six months. I usually try not to think about it, although occasionally it's kind of hard to ignore. Like a couple of months ago when I opened Liam's desk drawer to get a pen and I found a box of condoms. I told myself it didn't mean they were sleeping together, that Liam could be holding on to them just in case, like when they handed out condoms at school and all the guys took them to make it *seem* like they were having sex, even the ones who weren't.

But now that Izzy's confirming it, it's just another reminder that she has access to a part of Liam I don't, that no matter how much Liam and I talk about his music and his family and what he wants to do with his life and politics and millions of other things, she's the one he kisses, the one he touches, the one he apparently has sex with. And everyone knows that sex trumps everything.

"Is that . . . is that not normal for you guys?" I ask, not sure I really want to know the answer.

"Yes." She nods. "We have sex a lot. And lately he just . . . hasn't been interested." Her tears finally spill over, leaving shiny tracks on her cheeks. I wish she was at least an ugly crier, but even her crying is delicate.

"That doesn't mean he's cheating on you," I say. "Maybe it's just a normal settling down. Like how they say married couples don't have that much sex."

"But we're not married!"

"Yeah, but maybe it's not about being married, maybe it's just about being together for a while."

She shakes her head, almost like she wants to discount the possibility that everything could be okay, that their lack of sex is just something normal. "No," she says. "It's not just that. He's just been really distant lately. Have you noticed anything?"

"I mean, I've noticed we haven't been going over to his house as much, but I guess I didn't really think much of it." I rack my brain, trying to think if I've noticed Liam acting differently. I guess maybe he's been on his phone more. But has he really? Or am I just looking for things that aren't really there?

"You have to ask him," Izzy says, sounding desperate. "Please, Aven."

"No way," I say, shaking my head. "I can't do that."

"Why? He'll tell you. He tells you everything."

"No, he doesn't," I say, shaking my head. Still. I can't help feeling slightly flattered that she thinks Liam trusts me enough to tell me if he's cheating on her. "And besides, it's a no-win. If he tells me he isn't, you're just going to think he's lying so that I won't tell you. And if he tells me he is, then he's obviously going to ask me not to tell you. And if I do, he's going to know."

"No, you're right," she says. "I'm sorry, I shouldn't have put you in the middle like this."

"You didn't put me in the middle," I say, even though she kind of did.

"I just hate this," she says. "I love him so much."

It's the first time she's said the words out loud, at least to me. Do Izzy and Liam love each other? They've never said it in front of me. I wonder if these last little crumbs of hope I've clung to over the past six months—the fact that if they were really in love they would say it to each other, and that if they were really that serious, they'd be having sex—were just lies. They *have* been having sex. And now, according to Izzy, she loves him.

"I know," I say, even though I didn't until just now. I sigh and try to push my feelings for Liam out of my head. Izzy's my friend, and she's having a hard time, and I owe it to her to give her good advice, to tell her what she should do based on the facts at hand, not based on my own feelings for Liam. "Listen, Izzy, if you're worried about what's going on between you and Liam, you should ask him about it. Tell him you've felt a little bit of distance between you guys."

Izzy gives a delicate sniff, then dabs at her eyes with the corner of a piece of toilet paper. "Yeah," she says, giving me a smile. "You're right. I should just ask him."

"Good," I say. "I'm sure everything's fine. And once you guys talk, you'll feel a lot better."

"Thanks, Aven," Izzy says.

"You're welcome."

When Izzy and I walk out of the bathroom, I'm more con-fused than ever. For the past four years, I figured today would be the day I'd tell Liam how I really felt. But I never imagined that when this day came, he might be dating one of my friends. And I certainly never thought said friend would tell me she thought he was cheating on her.

Although I'm not sure the whole cheating thing makes much of a difference. If Liam *is* cheating on Izzy, does that mean he doesn't like her that much, so there might actually be a chance for me and him? Or does it mean he likes some other, faceless mistress so much that he wants to be with her more than either of us?

Do I even want to be with a guy who cheats? Is Liam even cheating? Maybe I should ask him. Or at least try to figure it out. There's no rule that says I have to tell Izzy, is there? Liam was my friend first. My allegiance should be to him. Shouldn't it? Or should it be to Izzy, since she's the one who approached me about it?

God, this is so confusing.

I hate the way I feel right now, and I'm starting to look at that email, which I always had positive feelings about, as my new enemy. I don't like the way it's playing with my emotions like some kind of puppet master—dance, emotions, dance! I don't like how it's, like, *pressuring* me.

God, I wish I could talk to someone about this.

But there are only two people who know about the email, only two people who know I love Liam. Two people who I miss more than anything, two people who I'm not speaking to, or actually, who aren't speaking to me.

Quinn and Lyla. My ex-best friends.

I wish I could ask one of them what to do.

I'm so caught up in my own thoughts that I don't even realize we're back in the boarding area now, and Izzy's looking at me expectantly, like she's waiting for me to say something.

"Do you?" she asks. "Want anything before we board?"

"Um, no," I say. "I'm okay."

Izzy disappears toward the food stands that are lining the walls of the airport, and I take a deep breath. I'm actually starting to feel pretty weird. My head is spinning, and it feels way too warm in here.

And that's when I spot Lyla, standing over by the wall near a row of chairs. I think about going over to talk to her. But then I remind myself that the last time I spoke to Lyla, she was screaming and telling me she wanted nothing to do with me. But still. This is an emergency. A mental one.

Before I can stop myself, I'm calling her name.

"Lyla! Lyla! There you are!" Even as the words are coming out of my mouth, I know they don't make any sense. I'm acting like I've been looking for her all over, when the truth is I just happened to spot her across the room. She's going to think I'm crazy for sure.

When she realizes it's me calling her name, a look of surprise crosses her face. But she doesn't look mad or anything, which I decide to take as a very good sign.

"Oh," she says. "Um . . . hi."

She seems confused. Good. This is good. If she's confused, I can just slip my question in before she realizes we're not speaking to each other, that she actually hates me. Although she really has no reason to hate me, because I didn't even do anything to her. In fact, our whole fight is just one big misunderstanding, if you ask me.

"Listen," I say, "I need to talk to you." I hold my phone up. I'm not sure why. Talking to her is making me nervous, and I'm afraid I'm not going to be able to get the words out without a visual aid. "Did you get your email?" I ask.

And then, for the first time, I realize she's with someone. Her boyfriend, Derrick. "Sorry," he says, shaking his head. He looks annoyed, like I'm some kind of bug that needs to be swatted away. "Aven, right? Sorry, Aven, but we're talking here. And it's kind of private."

Wow. What an asshole. Why is Lyla dating such a jerk?

My face flushes with embarrassment. "Oh," I say. "I'm sorry. I didn't . . . I mean, I didn't realize you were talking." This is the part where I should just walk away and leave them alone. Obviously I'm bothering them. Obviously Lyla doesn't want to talk to me. But it's my one chance to talk to someone about this, and I don't want to let it go. So I force myself to try again. "It's just . . . did you get your email?"

"My email?" Lyla repeats blankly.

"Yeah, the ones we sent? Did you get it?"

"What email?" Derrick asks, sounding all suspicious. Oh, good. Not only is he a jerk, he's one of those controlling guys who needs to know all about Lyla's internet activities. I want to give him a dirty look and tell him this is a private conversation, but obviously that's not going to work. No way Lyla's going to pick me over her jerk boyfriend.

"Yes," Lyla says to me. "I got it." I wait a beat, but she doesn't offer any more information. I force myself to wait, to see if she's going to say anything else. I know if I push her, she's going to shut down. That's how she is.

"Flight 935 to Sarasota is now boarding, Flight 935 to Sarasota is now boarding at Gate 24," a voice says over the loudspeaker.

"Well!" Lyla says, all fake-happy-like. "Here we go! I guess we better board."

"Where's your stuff?" Derrick asks her, frowning. "Didn't you bring a carry-on?"

"Nope," Lyla says. "Just this." She holds up her Coach wristlet, like she's daring one of us to question her. But her voice sounds a little bit strangled. Why wouldn't she bring a carry-on? We all got to check one suitcase, but pretty much everyone brought a carry-on anyway.

"That's all you brought for a carry-on?" I ask her skeptically. Lyla is usually an overpacker. When she'd come to my house for sleepovers she'd bring enough clothes to last a week.

"I'm trying to simplify my life," Lyla replies haughtily. "Everyone is so obsessed with materialism and *things*. I'm, you know, streamlining." She strokes her Coach wristlet like it's the only thing she needs to be happy in life.

Wow. She is acting really weird. I wonder if maybe she had some kind of mental breakdown or something after she stopped being friends with me and Quinn. Maybe that's why she hadn't wanted to talk to us. Because she was embarrassed by her mental illness.

"You're trying to streamline your life?" I ask carefully.

"A person can change," she says defiantly.

I shake my head. This conversation is getting really strange.

"When did you decide to simplify your life?" Derrick asks. "Because you never told me that." Great. Now he apparently needs to know every thought that goes through Lyla's head. Good luck with that, buddy. "Is this why you want to have sex?"

"You want to have sex?" I blurt before I can stop myself. Then I think about it. Of course they're going to have sex. They've been together for, like . . . at least a year or more. Why is it that Liam and Izzy are having sex after six months, but these two aren't? Do Liam and Izzy have some kind of crazy chemistry that can't be denied? Is Liam so attracted to her that he can't keep his hands off her no matter what? Hmmm. "Wait. You two haven't slept together yet? Haven't you been going out for forever?"

"Oh my God," Lyla says, sounding even more annoyed than Derrick. "Both of you need to stop."

For once, she's actually right. "Whatever," I say. "Your sex life is none of my business."

"You're damn right it's not," Lyla says, which is pretty harsh. I mean, I just admitted that her sex life wasn't any of my business, so why did she feel the need to point it out again?

This is not the way the conversation is supposed to be going. Lyla's not supposed to be getting irritated with me, she's supposed to be telling me what to do about my stupid email.

But before I can attempt to get the conversation back on track, Lyla turns around and starts walking away from me!

"Lyla," I say, trying to keep the desperation out of my voice. "Please, wait. Can we . . . I mean, can I talk to you for a second?"

She tilts her head and turns back around. "What is it?"

I glance at Derrick. I don't really want to get into this in front of him. He's too . . . like, nosy or something, and it's making me uncomfortable. "Um, I want . . . can we talk in private?"

She considers this, then sighs. "I'll be right back," she says to Derrick.

She walks a few feet away, and I follow her obediently. She crosses her arms over her chest, which is definitely not a very friendly posture. Yikes. "What is it?" she asks. "Make it quick, we're about to board."

I nod, then fiddle with the bottom of the fishtail braid I put my hair in this morning. "I just wanted to know if you're going to do what the email says."

"Excuse me?" Lyla asks, like she has no idea what I'm talking about, even though she just said a minute ago that she'd gotten her email. I remember exactly what she wrote, too. *Before graduation, I will . . . learn to trust.*

"Are you taking it seriously? You know, about learning to trust? Because I'm thinking . . . I'm thinking that I'm going to be really, um, trying to do what mine says." I try to sound more confident. "In fact, I've kind of been waiting for a chance to do it."

A look crosses her face, concern mixed with sadness. I know she's probably remembering what I wrote in my email. I also know she knows exactly what that means, that I'm going to tell Liam how I feel. She's probably wondering why

I haven't done it by now, why I've kept the secret this whole time, how it is that Liam and I could have remained so close all these years, when friendships can fall apart so easily, the way ours did.

I feel my heart soar for a second, wondering if she's going to tell me what to do, or at least give me some direction. Maybe at the very least she'll tell me what she's planning to do, and then I can do it, too.

But a second later, the soft look in her eyes is gone, replaced only by hardness.

"Yeah, Aven," she says sarcastically. "I'm really going to work on learning to trust. Because remember what happened when I trusted you? It didn't work out so well, remember?"

My face burns. "Lyla," I say. "I never wanted—"

"Save it," she says. "I didn't want to hear it then, and I don't want to hear it now."

She turns around and walks back to Derrick, leaving me standing there alone.

THREE

I SLEEP ON THE PLANE. THERE'S NOTHING
else to do, and like I've said, I've always found plane rides
soothing. I have a window seat in the row behind Izzy and
Liam, scrunched in next to two girls from my science class
who spend the whole ride trading magazines back and forth
and gossiping. I find their chatter soothing somehow, and it
lulls me to sleep.

I don't open my eyes until the plane is bouncing down
the runway in Sarasota. As soon as everyone's deplaned, they
rush us through the airport and onto a bus to take us to our
hotel, the Sand Dollar Siesta Hotel.

The sun is shining high in the sky as we walk into the
lobby, and it instantly brightens my mood. At least for a
minute, until my phone buzzes again and that stupid email
appears. After my nap, I'm thinking much more clearly
about this whole email nonsense, and so I delete it. I mean,

you don't just tell someone you're in love with them because of an email you sent yourself four years ago. If I want to tell Liam how I feel, it's not going to be because of some ambiguous deadline. There will be a right time to tell him, and when it happens, I'll just know.

But you thought the right time to tell him was going to be when you got that email.

Yeah, but I was mistaken.

You kept putting it off because you were waiting until you got that email, remember? It was like your deadline.

Deadlines are stupid.

Deadlines keep you from being a coward.

Hmm. I don't like that last thought. Am I a coward? Just because I won't tell Liam how I feel? I always told myself that email was like a built-in deadline, just in case I hadn't had a chance to tell him the truth. But is it realistic that in the four years we've been friends there was *no* good time to tell him how I really felt?

But there *wasn't*. He's with Izzy, for one. And yeah, only for like six months, but really, those six months would have been—

"Hey!" Liam says, popping up behind me.

"Hi!" I say, startled.

"Oh," he says, looking startled himself. "Sorry, didn't mean to scare you."

"You didn't scare me," I say as we join the throng of our

classmates filtering into the conference room on the first floor of the hotel. Before we're allowed to be let loose on Siesta Key, we have to sit through a presentation on all the rules of the trip.

"So, listen," Liam says, "I was thinking we should have a book club meeting while we're here."

"On our trip?"

"Sure," Liam says, grinning. "Why not? It might be fun to have book club on the beach."

"Did you finish the book?" I ask suspiciously. Liam and I started a book club a couple of years ago. We both love to read, but Liam is what I consider a book snob—he only looks for books that have won awards, or are about something of historical significance. You know, like about a Civil War soldier or something.

Not that there's anything wrong with that—I just always felt like maybe he was limiting himself with the kinds of books he gravitated toward. Of course he didn't agree, and he'd always tease me about the books I read, whether it was a mystery or a chick lit with a pink cover. So we decided to start a book club, where we switched off on picking the books—he always picks something literary and historical, and I always pick something fun and romantic.

"Yes," he says. "I finished it."

"You finished it?" I look at him incredulously. This month it was my pick, and I made him read this totally girly book called *Someday, Someday, Maybe*. It's about a girl trying to make it as an actress in New York City, so there's a lot of cool stuff about auditions and television shows, but there's also a love triangle with a really sexy actor and the girl's good-guy roommate. In other words, it's not really meant for a guy to read, much less a teenage guy.

"I did," Liam says, like he's shocked I would think otherwise. "And I can't wait to talk about it."

"Okay," I say. "Well, we can—"

But Izzy appears then, linking her arm through Liam's and resting her head on his shoulder. "That book club is so lame," she says. Liam threads his fingers through her hair and plays with the strands mindlessly. "Why do you guys want to torture yourselves by making each other read books you have no interest in?"

"We're trying to broaden our horizons," Liam explains.

"By reading chick lit and boring biographies?" Izzy sighs. "You guys should be broadening your horizons by seeing the world and having experiences."

I fight down a wave of annoyance that she's shitting all over books. Books *are* experiences. They *do* allow you to see the world, especially when you don't have the money or the opportunity to travel.

"We like book club," I say, and then, just because I feel like being annoying, I throw a little dig in. "Plus, it gives us a chance to bond."

Izzy sighs. "Well, whatever." She closes her eyes, and Liam smiles at her fondly and then kisses her on the head.

Ugh.

Our class adviser, Mr. Beals, tells us all to take a seat and settle down then. It takes him a while to get us all quiet, and then he starts going over all the rules for the trip. No drinking, no sneaking out, blah blah blah.

The rules are stupid and self-explanatory, and I already know them all because as part of the Student Action Committee, I got the chance to look over the list before it was made official. The administration wanted to make sure we thought the rules were fair. Which was ridiculous, because it wouldn't have mattered if we didn't—the school wasn't going to change anything.

Like I said, the Student Action Committee is a joke.

Of course, being on it does have some perks.

One of them being that I was in charge of creating the room assignments for this trip. Everyone had to fill out a questionnaire and list who they wanted to room with. All the rooms are triples, so you had to list your top three roommate choices. It was actually pretty easy to match people up, since mostly everyone had decided who they wanted to room with before they even filled out their form. So all I had to do was go through the forms and assign the room numbers. I had to do it by hand, which was ridiculous, since a simple computer program could have done it way faster. Everyone could have filled out their forms online and it would have taken just a few seconds for the computer to spit out the matches.

Instead I ended up in the library surrounded by forms, trying to enter everything into a stupid spreadsheet. Which was not fun. Especially since everyone was specifically told there could be no coed room assignments, and yet a few of the guys still listed girls on their forms. Some of them were dating, but some guys just picked random girls! Like I was going to be stupid enough to let them just sleep in the same room with girls they didn't even know. I mean, how creepy.

Also, a bunch of boys thought it would be hilarious to put random names down, like Godzilla, or Zac Efron or Jennifer Lawrence. But the joke was on them, because I just matched them all up randomly with people I was pretty sure they wouldn't get along with. Like, anyone who put down a funny name was immediately matched with someone who has an obvious hygiene problem. It wasn't even that hard—you'd be surprised how many boys my age have hygiene problems.

Of course, even though the whole thing was a pain in the ass, if we'd had to fill out our forms over the computer, then I'd never have been able to do what I did. Which was forge my room assignment. Actually, forge isn't the right word. That's only for signatures. It was more like I manipulated.

Manipulated myself right into rooming with Quinn and Lyla. They're probably going to go ballistic when they find out.

When Mr. Beals is done going over the rules, he starts droning on and on about the signs of ringworm and the fact that it's highly contagious. (Apparently someone brought it onto the bus with them, which is ridiculous—if you knew you had ringworm, why would you come on the trip? Talk about being totally irresponsible.) Great. Probably by the end of the trip everyone will have it.

I wonder what will happen if I end up with it. Maybe I'll have to be quarantined. Maybe Liam will have it, too, but somehow Izzy won't. We'll have to stay in our rooms, like when people get sick on cruise ships with norovirus and aren't allowed to leave their sleeping quarters. Obviously they'll have to make an exception to the whole no coed sleeping thing if people are sick.

Liam and I will end up sleeping in the same room, and of course we'll feel fine, we just won't be able to go anywhere because we won't be able to be around anyone. And we'll talk about that book *Someday, Someday, Maybe*, and I'll confess that I picked the book because I loved the title and it reminded me of him.

Actually, maybe I won't confess that. This is my fantasy, after all. And in my fantasy, shouldn't *Liam* be the one confessing his love to *me*? I can still use the book, though.

Only this time Liam will say the reason he liked the book so much and read it so fast was because he liked the title, that it reminded *him* of *me*. That he was just sort of sowing his wild oats with Izzy and—actually, no I don't like that. It makes it seem like maybe he wanted to use her for sex, like she was just so irresistible that he couldn't stay away from her, and now that he got what he wanted, he's done with her. Which isn't exactly the kind of guy you want appearing in your fantasies.

But then how am I supposed to explain the fact that he wanted Izzy over me? I'm not sure what's worse—that he just had a physical connection to her, or that he actually liked her.

Sigh.

"You coming?" I realize Liam's asking me. I look around. Everyone's gathering their things. The presentation must be over. No one looks too worried about ringworm. I hope that doesn't mean they're going to be reckless with their germ prevention measures.

"Oh," I say. "Yeah, sorry."

"What's your room number?" he asks me as we all filter back into the lobby.

"Two seventeen," I say. I don't even have to look at the paper they gave us when we got on the bus to the airport. I already know exactly what room I'm in, because I'm the one who assigned it.

"Cool," he says. "So what should we do after this? You wanna hit the beach?"

"What about Izzy?" I ask. "What's she doing?"

He shrugs. "She has something planned with her dance team," he says.

"Oh." I swallow hard. "Okay."

Liam and me.

Alone on the beach.

The perfect time to tell him.

Now all I have to do is make sure I really want to go through with it.

FOUR

IT'S GOING TO BE FINE.

I just have to think positive.

I'm a big believer in the theory that your attitude can influence what's going to happen to you. So I just have to make sure I'm putting bright energy out into the world and everything will be okay. Including the fact that Lyla, Quinn, and I are about to be in the same room for the first time in over two years.

I take the elevator up to the second floor, and when I step off, I can see Quinn down the hall, wrestling her bag through the door of our room before it closes behind her. As I get closer, I can hear voices coming from inside. Lyla must already be there.

I press my ear to the door, trying to see if I can make out what they're saying. But while everything else in the hotel is light and airy, the doors are made of dark oak. I can't hear much of anything, except a few tense-sounding mumbles. And then nothing. Hmm. Silence really isn't a good sign. Silence means they're not talking. And if they're not talking, how are they going to make up? I'm not stupid enough to think we're all going to mend our issues with a few minutes of conversation, but we might be able to get things headed in the right direction.

I mean, shouldn't they at least be discussing little things, like where to put the suitcases or how nice the hotel is? What about the weather? Even strangers talk about the weather! Have the three of us gotten to the point that we're not even able to treat each other the way we'd treat *strangers*?

A memory flashes—the three of us standing outside school, Lyla yelling. Quinn and I standing there, dazed, not really able to believe what was happening. I pause with my key card over the door, wondering for the first time if this was a stupid plan, if maybe I should head back downstairs and ask Mr. Beals if there's any way to change the room assignments.

But I miss them so much.

I can't talk to anyone else the way I could talk to them.

Yes, I have Liam, but he's a boy.

And Izzy is a girl, but she's Liam's girlfriend, which makes it impossible to ever be close to her the way you should be with someone who's supposed to be a best friend. Izzy can never truly know me, because the way I feel about Liam is a big part of my life, and I can't ever share that with her.

And if I'm being completely honest, even if Izzy *wasn't* dating Liam, I don't think we'd be the kind of friends that me and Lyla and Quinn were. Lyla and Quinn and I just got (get?) each other. They were the kind of friends you could call at three in the morning or one in the afternoon. The kind of friends who, when you showed up to their houses unannounced, their parents were happy to see you and sent you right up to their rooms. The kind of friends who didn't even finish each other's sentences, because a lot of times we didn't even need to talk—we could tell what the others were thinking just by looking at each other.

But all that is gone now.

And I want it back.

I want it back so much it *hurts*.

And I'm not going to give up.

I slide my key card into the door and walk into the room, a smile pasted on my face. It's not even fake. I know it sounds super cheesy, but I'm just so happy to see the two of them here, together, in the same room that I can't help myself.

Lyla's sitting on one of the beds, looking a little stunned. Quinn's standing by the dresser, unpacking her stuff. Her bag is sitting on the other bed.

I glance around the room until my eyes land on the cot in the corner. Well. Apparently these two got here and grabbed the beds, leaving me with the cot. I try to muster up the energy to be mad at them for not waiting for me so we could decide about the beds together. But I can't. I'm just so happy that the three of us are all together that the anger flows out of my body in one swoosh.

"I guess I'm taking the cot," I say happily. I drop my stuff onto it, and the cot creaks in protest. The mattress is paper-thin and sagging in the middle. Hmm. *Good energy,* I remind myself. *Good energy, good energy, good energy.*

Quinn and Lyla are staring at me expectantly, like they're waiting for me to complain. Either that, or they know I put us all in the same room. It wouldn't be that hard to figure out. I mean, obviously they know they requested to room with other people.

Quinn, for instance, wrote down Celia Grant and Paige Whitman. Those are her friends now, which is ridiculous if you ask me. Those two are the biggest jerks, like, in the school. Everyone knows it. Not to mention they're total pill heads. There was a rumor going around not that long ago about Celia and Paige wandering all over Hartford one night looking to buy Valium. I mean, it was never substantiated, but still. If Quinn can be friends with those two, why can't she be friends with me and Lyla again?

They're still looking at me.

"I think we could all benefit from spending some time together," I say, hoping my tone sounds light and upbeat. I'm trying to go for an unpressured way of speaking, but as soon as the words are out of my mouth, I realize they sound kind of stiff, the kind of thing you'd say if you were a married couple having problems, not three best friends trying to reconnect on their senior trip. "I know that our misunderstanding got out of hand, but with graduation coming up, I think it might really be time to move past it."

Also a weird thing to say. How can we just move past it? The three of us haven't talked in years. I should have planned this out better. I'm obviously horrible at talking off-the-cuff.

Should I plan out what I'm going to say to Liam if I decide to tell him how I feel? I thought it would be better if the moment was natural, but now I'm starting to think that might be a complete disaster.

Lyla gives a bitter little laugh. "That's what you think it was? A misunderstanding?"

Well, yeah. Kind of. Not to discount Lyla's feelings or anything, but what happened between the three of us wasn't that big of a deal. It was serious, but not serious enough to end our friendship.

"I know your feelings are still probably really hurt, Lyla," I say. "But Quinn and I never meant to hurt you."

"Don't speak for me," Quinn says.

I frown. What the hell is wrong with her? Why would she dispute what I just said, that the two of us never meant to hurt Lyla? What a dumb thing to contradict.

"So you did mean to hurt me?" Lyla says. Sigh.

"Whatever," Quinn says, shaking her head. "I don't want to do this. I don't even care about this. It takes up, like, this amount of space in my mind." She holds her fingers up the tiniest bit apart, to show just how little she thinks of it. I want to say something like, *Ah, but you do think about it a little*, but before I can, Quinn turns and walks out of the room!

Then the door opens back up and she pokes her head in. She looks right at me, her eyes boring into my soul. "Keep your hands off my stuff, Aven," she says. "I know you like to borrow people's things."

She gives me this really fake smile before disappearing back through the door. Wow. I cannot *believe* she said that. I mean, talk about a low blow. Just because one time I had to go into her gym locker to borrow some clothes. It was the day we had to run the mile, and I didn't have any gym clothes, and if I hadn't taken hers I would have had to run the mile on makeup day. And I hate running the mile on makeup day, because then you have to do it after school with, like, the boys' track team. It's humiliating to plod around the track running a ten-minute mile while they all run in the sixes.

And besides, I put Quinn's clothes right back in her locker. It's not my fault I didn't realize I'd gotten orange Gatorade on her shorts. I needed a drink after I was done running because I'd forgotten to hydrate properly and I started feeling all dizzy.

For a second, I feel like I'm going to cry.

I turn to look at Lyla.

"Lyla," I plead. "Can we just—"

She holds her hand up, stopping me. "No. Let's make this easy. I didn't want to forgive you then, and I still don't want to forgive you now. So save whatever dumb thing you're about to say."

I feel like I've been slapped. And then, a split second later, I realize how stupid I've been. How could I have thought that the three of us would be able to be friends again just by being roommates on this dumb trip? The fight between us was so bad—whether I think it was justified or not—that just staying in the same room isn't going to make everything magically better.

Suddenly, I'm mad.

Mostly at myself.

But also at Lyla.

"Forget it," I say to Lyla. "Just forget it. I was stupid to think that maybe you'd changed even a little bit."

"Me?" she asks incredulously. "I'm the one who has to change?"

Is she serious? Of course she's the one who has to change! Quinn and I didn't even do anything wrong! All we were doing was being there for her, trying to help her. And she just completely went off on us and didn't even try to listen to our side of the story.

Who does that? Our friendship was so deep, and she just turned around and in the blink of an eye, totally made it seem like it meant nothing to her. Because if it had, wouldn't she have at least tried to talk to us, to listen to us, to try to understand? But she didn't. She just decided she was right because it was easier. It was easier to blame us than to face what was really going on and try to work through it.

"You don't get it, Lyla," I say. "You really don't. In fact, you're just as selfish as you used to be."

There's nothing left to say.

So I follow Quinn's lead, and turn and walk out.

Except unlike Quinn, I slam the door behind me.

And I don't come back.

Whatever. I don't even care about Quinn and Lyla. I was a good friend to both of them, and if they think I'm going to let them ruin my vacation, well then, they have another thing coming.

Although now that I'm standing outside in the hallway, I'm not exactly sure what it is I'm supposed to do. So I text Liam.

Meet me in the lobby?

Thank God I wore my Florida outfit on the plane—a long-sleeved T-shirt and shorts, with my bathing suit underneath it. At the time I thought it might have been a little ridiculous, but now I'm thankful I don't have to spend another minute in that room.

I head for the elevator, jamming the button for the lobby angrily.

Those two! I can't believe I ever thought that the three of us could be friends again. The two of them are obviously completely unhinged. I mean, who talks like that to people they used to be friends with?

Good riddance to the both of them! They are not the kind of friends I want! Of course, our fight must have been really hard on Lyla, with what was going on at the time. I mean, her parents were getting divorced. And it must have been pretty upsetting for the two of them to think they were rooming with their friends on this trip and then realize I'd abused my power so that the three of us would end up together. I'd probably be mad, too.

So maybe when everyone's had a chance to just calm down a little bit, then—

"Aven! There you are!"

I'm in the lobby now, and Izzy's there for some reason, calling my name. She's changed into a cute aqua sundress and strappy tan sandals, her hair in a ponytail.

"Oh," I say, confused. "Sorry, were we supposed to meet down here? Did Liam invite you? I thought you had something to do with your dance team."

"I did. I do. I just thought maybe you'd have texted me or

something. You know, after what I told you." She raises one eyebrow. Seriously, just one. Izzy can do that. It's, like, one of her talents.

"Oh," I say, uncomfortable. "Sorry, I thought you'd kind of moved on."

"Moved on from Liam cheating on me?" She shakes her head like she can't believe how ridiculous that is. Which it kind of is. I guess what I meant was that I was *hoping* she'd move on from it. But obviously I can't say that. "I really don't think so."

"Okay," I say. I'm not sure what she wants me to do.

"Anyway," she says, looking over her shoulder to where the dance team is in a loose huddle by the door. "The dance team is going for lunch. It's, like, part of our dancing."

I don't know what she's talking about. How can going to lunch be part of their dancing? "How is going to lunch part of your dancing?"

"It helps us foster a sense of trust with each other, which helps when we do our lifts."

I hope they have a really long lunch, then. The dance team performs during halftime at most of the basketball games, and at the last game they threw Raven Marsden up into some kind of throw and almost didn't catch her on the way down. Also, one time their pyramid leaned to the side and then just collapsed. I really don't think they should be doing moves like that unless they can guarantee the safety of all the students involved. The last thing the school needs is someone bashing their head open all over the gym floor in front of everyone. You just know it would end up on You-Tube, too. Hmm. I wonder if this is something I should bring up with the Student Action Committee.

"Anyway, I have to go," Izzy says. "But I really need you to do something for me."

She glances around like she's afraid someone's going to hear us. Which makes me nervous. Anytime someone's asking you to do something for them and then looking around like they don't want anyone else to hear, it can't be good. No one cares about eavesdropping over something benign like, *Oh, can you pass me the pepper?* or *Can you help me with my calculus?*

"What?" I ask warily.

"I know I said I didn't want to put you in the middle, but can you please try to find out what's going on with Liam?" she asks. "Just . . . I mean, I know you don't want to come right out and ask him, but can you just . . . sort of, like, hint and see if he's been talking to someone else?"

"Izzy," I say carefully. "If you're worried about Liam, I think you should just ask him what's going on. Seriously, it's not—"

"Please, Aven," she pleads. She grabs my arm and her fingers dig into my flesh. It actually kind of hurts. "You're the only one I can turn to for help. You know I wouldn't ask if it wasn't important."

"I know, Izzy, but—"

"Just see what you can find out, okay?"

"Okay." The word slips out of my mouth before I can stop it. Of course I'm not going to try and see what I can find out. First of all, it's kind of none of my business. And second of all, why would I want to know if Liam is cheating on Izzy? I'm having enough trouble with him *liking* Izzy. Now I'm going to have to find a completely new girl to have to deal with? No way.

I'll just tell Izzy I couldn't find out anything.

She probably won't even care that much. She just wants to vent and feel like someone cares.

"Thanks, Aven," Izzy says. "You're the best."

She turns around and walks away, her ponytail swishing behind her. I watch as she meets up with her dance team, all of them with the same long ponytails and toned bodies.

I shake my head.

I can't believe Izzy's worried about Liam cheating on her. No one would cheat on Izzy. She's just too damn perfect.

Welcome to my life.

Of course, good-looking people get cheated on all the time. I mean, look at Beyoncé and Jay-Z. Everyone says he cheated. And Beyoncé's beautiful and rich and amazing. So Liam *could* be cheating on Izzy. Not that I think Liam's the type to do something like that. Of course, I'm definitely biased.

I glance at him out of the corner of my eye, trying to see if I can spot anything different about him.

It's half an hour or so later, and we're walking down Ocean Boulevard, looking for a place to grab some snacks we can eat during book club on the beach. He doesn't look like the kind of guy who's cheating or harboring any kind of secret.

In fact, he looks even more relaxed than he usually does. He's wearing his Brookline Lacrosse hat, the one he spent days working on so he could get the brim to fold just right. He's walking fast, the way he usually does, his strides so long I'm almost struggling to keep up.

He needs a haircut. I can see the back of his hair sort of peeking through the back of his baseball cap. Hmm. That doesn't seem like the kind of thing a guy cheating on someone would do, does it? If he was with some new girl, wouldn't he be keeping up with his hair in an effort to impress her? Or maybe she likes it long, so he's growing it out.

"Your hair's getting long," I say nonchalantly.

"Yeah," he says. "I know. You want to cut it for me later?"

"What?"

"Yeah." He pulls his hat off and runs his fingers through it. "It's too hot to keep my hair like this."

"You trust me to cut your hair?"

"What's the worst that can happen?"

"Um, I screw it all up and you end up looking ridiculous."

"Good thing I already got my senior pictures done, then." He looks over and smiles at me. "You won't screw it up. And if you do, I'll just shave my head."

Hmm. A guy who was cheating definitely wouldn't trust me to cut his hair and then shave his head if it didn't work out. Although Liam doesn't usually get all worked up about things like that. So maybe this new girl just likes him for himself.

I start to run through a list of girls in my class who it could be. Karli Karlson? Jada Ryan? Rhiannon Joy? Then I realize I'm acting crazy. Just because Izzy thinks Liam is cheating on her doesn't mean he is. That's ridiculous. Liam wouldn't cheat. If he didn't want to be with Izzy anymore, he would just break up with her.

I don't think it's my bias talking, either. Yes, I'm in love with Liam. But I'm not under the illusion that he's perfect. He's not. He gets cranky when he doesn't have enough sleep, he sometimes lets his dad push him into doing things he doesn't want to do, and he can be lazy about school stuff. There are a million things Liam isn't perfect at, but he's not a cheater. I need to stop letting Izzy get into my head.

A few minutes later we pass an ice-cream shop called Big Olaf, and we stop for cones even though neither one of us has had anything resembling real food since this morning. Another one of Liam's flaws—he eats processed sugar whenever he can.

Although that's not really a flaw—why should it be when his body is still insane? Seriously, I've seem Liam without a shirt a fair amount of times—at the pool, after his games, at the end of a 10K he ran. His stomach is flat and toned, with a perfect six-pack, and his arms are defined in all the right places. So obviously the processed sugar isn't hurting him much.

After we get our cones (chocolate chip cookie dough for me, and a double scoop of chocolate brownie for him) we head to the beach. We find an open spot on the sand and lay out the Siesta Key beach blanket we bought at a souvenir stand. It cost us forty dollars. For a blanket! Another one of Liam's flaws—he spends money like crazy and doesn't really think about it.

And it's not like his family is rich or anything, either. Liam even had to get an after-school job at Dick's Sporting Goods so he could save money for college. Which obviously he's not doing if he's spending forty dollars on a blanket.

He's probably going to be broke soon. I try to imagine a future where I'm married to Liam, and he's taken all our money and spent it on something frivolous, like a huge flat-screen TV. Our children would end up hungry. Or eating nothing but cheap packaged snacks filled with high fructose corn syrup.

Our children would be so cute, though. We'd have three boys. I don't want any girls. They seem like they would be too much to handle. And boys really look to their dad to handle all of the hard stuff. I'll bet Liam would be so good at that. He's so patient and kind. He'd be a great dad, especially after the way his own dad is so hard on him. Liam always said he wouldn't want to be that way with his kids, that he'd let them make their own decisions and not put any kind of pressure on them.

He'd be—wait. How did Liam spending all his money and eating processed foods and possibly cheating on his girlfriend turn into a fantasy about how he'd be a great dad?

Gah!

"So let's talk about the book," Liam says.

"Okay." I take a lick of my ice-cream cone and wait for what I know is coming.

"I hated that book."

It's the way we start every single book club. Whoever picked the book sits there patiently until the other person says, *So let's talk about the book,* and then you're supposed to reply, *Okay,* and then the person who had to read the book you picked says, *I hated that book.*

"No, you didn't," I say.

"Yes, I did." Liam's already almost done with his ice-cream cone, even though he had two scoops and I only had one. "It was ridiculous."

"What was ridiculous about it?"

"The ending!" he says, taking the last bite of his cone.

He chews and swallows before talking again. "There was all that buildup, you know, about how she was trying to make it as an actress and how she'd set this weird deadline for herself, and then at the end, it just . . . sort of ended. Like you didn't know if she made it or not."

"Well, obviously she did!"

"It didn't say that, though." Liam turns his hat around until it's backward and then tilts his face toward the sun.

"You should be wearing sunscreen," I say, shaking my head. "You're going to burn."

"But I need my vitamin D," he says. "You should have ten to fifteen minutes a day of sunshine with no sunscreen."

"Says who?"

"Dr. Oz."

I frown. "Really?"

"Yeah."

"Since when did you start watching Dr. Oz?" Maybe his new girlfriend watches it. Maybe all those times Liam claimed to be working on his music he was really holed up somewhere watching Dr. Oz. Not that Dr. Oz is on late night. But maybe he DVRs a bunch of them and then the new girl comes over and they cuddle up in bed and watch episode after episode. Like a marathon. I wonder what Dr. Oz has to say about ordering a double chocolate brownie ice-cream cone and downing it in three seconds.

Liam shrugs. "My mom had it on."

I shake my head. "Anyway, back to the book." I take a delicate lick of my ice-cream cone, trying to make sure I'm not hoovering it down while still trying to keep up with it enough so that it doesn't drip down my arm. "She *did* make it at the end. She was getting all those auditions and work."

"Yeah, but she hadn't had her big break, though. We didn't know for sure it was going to work out."

"That was the point! It was all about the journey."

"But you just said that of course it worked out, that she made it."

"She did."

"How do you know?"

"Because she was gaining momentum!"

Liam shakes his head. "If you say so." He looks over at me and gives me a sly grin. "What did you think about the romance?"

"What did *you* think about the romance?" I counter. Liam has this crazy idea that I need to have a romance in a book to truly enjoy it. Which isn't true. I just think that romance adds something to books, because let's face it—love and romance are a huge part of life. They trump almost everything else. That's why you always hear about people with power and celebrity and money being brought to their knees by a new love or an affair or a divorce. Love really does make the world go round.

"I thought it was ridiculous," Liam says. "Why was she

with that guy? The actor guy who was getting famous?"

"Um, because he was hot and a famous actor?"

"Yeah, but he was such a douche. And the guy who really liked her, Dan? He was so nice, and he seemed interesting. He was a writer. I wanted to see more of them together."

"But they did end up together at the end," I point out.

"Yeah, after she'd wasted the whole book with that other guy."

I take in a deep breath, wondering how Liam can so clearly see the wrongness of a romance in a book, and yet can't tell the wrongness in his romantic life right now. I mean, what he's saying is the same exact thing that's happening to him *in real life*. Why does he want to be with Izzy when he could be with me? I mean, yeah, she's prettier than me. And I'm not saying that to be self-deprecating or whatever. It's just a fact. She has long blond hair, and her body is perfect from all the dancing she does. But that's all she has over me when it comes to Liam.

Liam and I have more in common.

We talk more.

We're just . . . better.

So how can he sit there and tell me about the romance being wrong in that book when he's living out the exact same thing? Unless . . . maybe he's trying to give me some kind of hint.

"Well, yeah," I say slowly. "But sometimes we need a little

help, you know, figuring out what's right for us. Like who we should end up with."

"I guess." He shrugs. "But that guy was so obviously wrong for her."

"They had sexual chemistry," I say, before I realize that might not be the best thing to bring up. Although if Liam and Izzy aren't having sex much, maybe their sexual chemistry has been dampened a bit.

"So what?" he says. "Sexual chemistry fades out."

I lick my ice-cream cone and think about what he's saying. I can't imagine my attraction to Liam fading out. Every time he's around me, my stomach does somersaults, my skin prickles, and my heart does a weird little dance.

He turns to look at me, his blue eyes bright and serious. He's staring at me. Now's the moment. Now's the time I should tell him how I feel. It's the perfect segue.

I'll tell him that it's important you have a good friendship with the person you end up with, just like Franny did in the book. That it might have taken her a while to realize it, that she might have spent a lot of time with the wrong person because she was blinded by lust or bad decisions, but all that matters is who you end up with, not how you got there.

"Liam," I say, taking a deep breath. *Just do it. Do it. It's just Liam. You have to know. You have to do it.*

"Yeah?" he asks.

My mouth goes dry. *Go on. Tell him.*

"Oh God, Aven, your ice cream," he says.

I look down. It's dripping all down my arm, leaving a sticky trail on my skin. "Oh," I say, surprised.

Liam laughs and takes my cone from me, licking it until it's fixed. He takes his napkin, which he's hardly touched, and wipes my arm until the melted ice cream is gone.

"Thanks," I say.

He holds the cone back out to me, but I shake my head. "You can have it."

"You sure?"

"Yeah, I just . . . I'm not hungry anymore."

"You okay?"

"Yeah, I'm fine."

He looks at me. "No, you're not."

"Yes, I am."

"No, you're not. Tell me what's wrong."

"Nothing! I swear."

"You know you're going to end up telling me eventually," he says confidently. And he's right. At least, he would be if we were talking about anything else. He's the first person I tell about whatever's going on with me, good or bad. When Lyla and Quinn and I had our fight, I spent, like, three days at Liam's house, curled up on his bed, moaning about how sad and lonely I was. When I was sick of talking about it, I'd crawl under his covers and watch Netflix documentaries or read books while he worked on his music and brought me snacks.

But this is different.

The one thing I want to tell him is the one thing I can't.

"Are you upset because I didn't like the book? Because I'm just joking, Aven. I mean, I did like it. Parts of it, anyway. It wasn't a bad pick. Definitely not as bad as *Baby Proof*."

I elbow him playfully. "No," I say. "I'm not upset about the book."

"Good, because—"

"Yo, Marsh!" a voice comes from down the beach.

Liam and I look up to see one of his friends from soccer, Miles Wentmore, walking toward us. He's wearing board shorts and no shirt, tossing a football back and forth between his hands.

"Hey, Miles," Liam says. I'm not sure, but I think he sounds kind of annoyed. Is he annoyed? Is he upset that Miles is interrupting our book club?

"Come on, we're playing catch," Miles instructs, in the way that only very cocky, good-looking guys can do.

"I'm kind of tired," Liam says.

"Oh, come on, don't be a pussy," Miles says. He's tossing the ball faster now, like showing off will somehow convince Liam to do what Miles wants.

Liam glances over at me, questioning.

"Don't stay because of me," I say, holding my hands up.

"Are you sure? I mean, we're kind of in the middle of something."

"It's fine." It is, but it isn't. I don't really care that Liam is going to throw the ball around with his friends, but at the same time, I don't want him to leave, either. But it's not like I have a right to be selfish about it—I've never had to fight Liam to spend time with him. In fact, it's kind of the opposite. He's usually accessible to me, always there when I need him, always wanting to be around me. But that's what makes everything so horribly confusing. If he's spending more time with me than with Izzy, if he's so happy to just sit and talk about a chick-lit book with me, then why aren't we together?

"You're the best, Aven," Liam says. He stands up and brushes the sand off his shorts, then reaches down and grabs the bottom of his T-shirt, pulling it up and over his head. I catch my breath. Seeing Liam shirtless is a completely different experience from seeing Miles without his. Although it could be argued that Miles has the better body, with his eight-pack and smooth, perfectly tan skin, Liam is definitely hotter.

He's lean, and his six-pack sits perfectly above the waistband of his shorts, which are sitting so low on his hips that he has to reach down and hitch them up, tying the drawstring tighter. A thin line of hair starts at his belly button and slides down out of sight. He tosses his shirt at me, hitting me in the face with it. "You're in charge of that," he says.

"Eww," I say, throwing the shirt back at him. "What makes you think I want to take care of your smelly shirt?"

He gives it a sniff. "It's not smelly," he says. "It's perfectly clean."

"No, it's not," I say. "You're a boy. Boys are dirty."

"Aven," Liam says patiently, the way he does when he's pretending he's exasperated with me even though he really isn't. I love when he does that, love the way my name sounds coming out of his mouth, like it's not just my name, but something special he calls me. "I'm a very clean person."

"Right," I say, rolling my eyes, even though it's true. Liam's very clean. Well, for a boy. He always showers and uses Axe body spray. I know because one time I saw it in his bathroom. Not to mention how good he smells.

"Come on," Miles whines. "Are you coming or not?"

"I'll watch your shirt," I say to Liam, and he tosses it back to me. "But it's going to cost you something."

"What?"

"Rent."

"How much?"

"Marsh! Stop flirting and come on," Miles says.

Miles thinks Liam and I are flirting! Are we flirting? Do we flirt? "I'll see you later, back at the hotel?" Liam asks.

"Sure," I say. "See you back at the hotel."

I sit there for a minute, watching the two of them disappear down the beach.

My phone buzzes.

Before graduation, I will . . . *tell the truth.*

I sigh. Fourteen-year-old me thought that seventeen-year-old me would have it all figured out, some great plan for how to tell Liam the truth, some great strategy for dealing with whatever he said, good or bad. Poor, naive fourteen-year-old me. I almost feel sorry for her.

I stand up and take a deep breath, closing my eyes and feeling the sun on my face, listening to the roar of the ocean and the call of the seagulls.

Then I turn around and start walking back toward the hotel.

Sorry, fourteen-year-old me. Seventeen-year-old me is just as confused as you are.

I haven't walked far when, out of nowhere, I feel someone grab me around the legs.

"You didn't think you'd get off that easy, did you?" Liam says.

I giggle as he picks me up like a sack of potatoes and throws me over his shoulder. "Put me down!" I cry. "What are you doing?"

He's running down the beach with me slung over his

body, moving easily like I'm as light as a feather.

"We're doing sword fights," he explains, placing me back on the sand.

My hair flops into my face, and I push it back, then take a step forward. The blood has all rushed to my head, and it's making me feel a little dizzy.

"You're doing what?" I ask, confused.

"We're having sword fights. You know, in the water?"

"That doesn't . . . you mean *crab* fights?" Crab fights make way more sense than sword fights. Crab fights are when a guy takes a girl and puts her on his shoulders, then another couple stands across from them, and the two girls try to push each other off and into the water. Whoever stays on their partner's shoulders wins. I've never done it before, but I saw it on an episode of *The Office*. It was a really funny episode, where everyone from the office goes to their boss's house and—wait. If Liam and Miles are going to have a crab fight, does that mean . . . does Liam expect me to get on his shoulders?

"Yeah, crab fights." Liam leans in toward me. "Miles spotted Skye Walker on the beach, and so that's what he wants to do now." He lowers his voice. "This could be a big problem for us, because there are certain areas of her body you might need to avoid."

I grin. Skye Walker has fake boobs, a present from her parents for graduation, which actually didn't make any sense since she got her surgery last summer. If it was for graduation, shouldn't her parents have actually waited until she graduated? But Skye said she didn't want to spend the summer before college recovering, that she needed time to get used to her new body.

She was actually very open about the whole thing, not like Mila Thompson, who showed up on the first day of school with a brand-new nose and tried to deny she'd had any work done even though it was completely obvious.

"I don't think that's how it works," I say. "I don't think I can pop her boob."

"Who said anything about popping it?" Liam asks, aghast. "I just meant she might still be sore there."

"From, like, a year ago?" I shake my head. "I doubt it. And even if—"

"We're going to crush you guys!" Miles yells. He's already waded a few feet into the water, and he kicks up some of the spray. "You're going down, Marsh!"

Skye's just standing there on the shore, giggling. I like Skye. I don't know her that well, but she's always been nice to me. She hangs out with the popular girls, but she's low on their totem pole. It's like she knows they're ridiculous, but she can't not hang out with them because she's so pretty that there's no way she can't be popular.

"Hey, Aven," she says.

"Hi, Skye."

"This is stupid," someone calls from the sand.

I turn to look. Jillian Colangelo and Grace Smythe are lying on the beach on their stomachs, their bikinis undone in the back as they tan themselves.

"You're going to get your hair all wet," Grace says to Skye.

"So?" Skye says, like she doesn't understand what the big deal is.

"If you get your hair all wet, then you'll have to dry it," Jillian says.

"No, I won't," Skye says. "The sun will dry it."

"Yeah, if you want to look like a frizz head," Grace mutters.

"What's your problem?" Skye asks. "You were just saying that you wanted to play!"

"That was when I thought Liam needed a partner," Grace says. "But I wouldn't just, like, do it for no reason."

"That doesn't make any sense," Skye says.

"Whatever." Grace rolls her eyes and then expertly flips herself over to tan her front. She holds her bathing suit top over her chest as she does so, somehow able to keep everything covered.

"You didn't tell me you already had a partner," I say to Liam, trying to keep my voice neutral. Did Liam turn Grace down just so he could be partners with me? Why else would he chase me down the beach when Grace was ready and willing to climb onto his shoulders?

"Sorry," he says. "You don't mind, do you? I mean, you know, with Izzy . . ." He trails off.

And then I get it. If he'd gone into the water with Grace, who is arguably one of the prettiest girls in our class, it might have been seen as inappropriate. There's something really flirty about climbing onto a guy's shoulders and trying to push another girl around—it seems almost sexual, in an animalistic kind of way.

If Izzy had found out Liam had been splashing around the water with Grace in her string bikini, she wouldn't have been pleased. But with me, it's different. I'm safe. I'm non-threatening. Izzy has never been threatened by me because there's no need to be—I knew Liam way before she did. If anything was going to happen between us, it would have happened by now.

"Oh," I say. "No, I mean . . . I don't mind playing."

But of course I do. Now that I know I'm just being slotted into this game because I'm seen as nonthreatening, I don't want to play. But what can I do? If I tell Liam I changed my mind, it's going to seem really weird.

So I slide out of my shorts and drop them on the sand, then pull my T-shirt over my head. The light-blue tankini I'm wearing underneath seems completely lame compared to the bathing suits the other girls are wearing. Skye's bikini is held together at the sides by two tiny string bows that look like they're about two seconds away from coming undone. And the material hardly covers her butt.

It said in the informational packet the school sent out that no one was allowed to bring inappropriate bathing suits. Which is why I bought this stupid tankini! But apparently no one else really cared about what was allowed. Either that or they have a very different idea of what constitutes inappropriate.

Probably both.

"Come on," Miles says. "We're going to kill you guys."

"No need for violence," Liam says. He's wading into the ocean, and I follow him, almost gasping as the water hits my shins. It's freezing.

Oh, well. More incentive not to get pushed off Liam's shoulders. Not that I'm too worried about it. I outweigh Skye by about twenty-five pounds, and anyone who would stay in the popular group when it obviously makes her miserable probably doesn't have much of a fighting spirit. So I think I've got this.

Once we're in the water, Miles reaches down and hoists Skye up onto his shoulders.

I look at Liam.

Liam looks at me.

Then he sort of crouches down, and I awkwardly climb onto him.

Oh. My. God.

I am on Liam's shoulders. I thought it would feel weird, being up here, and scary, because I'm so off the ground, but it doesn't. Instead, I feel safe. Liam's grip on my ankles is strong, and his body feels sturdy beneath me. My pulse races.

"Okay, Skye," Miles instructs. "Get her."

He starts charging toward us.

When they get within reach, Skye and I just look at each other. "This is awkward," I say.

"Yeah," she says, giving me a tiny little smile.

"Come on," Miles whines. "Push each other off."

"I just . . . it seems kind of mean," Skye says.

"Yeah," I agree, dropping my arms slightly. "How am I supposed to—" But I don't get to finish my sentence, because Skye picks that moment to pounce. She grabs my wrists and starts to try and wrestle me off Liam's shoulders.

"Hey!" I protest. "That wasn't fair. I wasn't ready."

"You snooze, you lose," she says gleefully.

"Let go!" I yell, which is more like a reflex than anything I expect is really going to work. Of course she's not going to let go. The whole point of the game is to hold on.

But surprisingly, she loosens her grip. "Sorry," she says. "Was I hurting you?"

"You snooze, you lose," I say, and then I push her as hard as I can. It's surprisingly ineffective. Her upper body slides back a little bit, but it's nowhere near enough to knock her off Miles's shoulders.

"You guys really suck at this," Miles says.

"Give them a break," Liam says. "They're the ones doing all the hard work."

"Dude, if I was up there, I guaran-fucking-tee you I would have had your ass dumped into the water by now," Miles says.

"Doubtful," Liam says. "You might be strong, but you have no real agility. No offense."

"Oh, none taken," Miles says. He raises his head so he can look right at Liam, and Skye's body weight shifts back just a little bit, so that she's farther back on his shoulders. I take the chance and pounce. But she's ready. She grabs my arms as I push her, and in a brilliant move, instead of going against me and trying to push me back, she pulls me toward her, using all my momentum to throw me off balance.

"Hold me tight!" Skye screams at Miles, and he does.

A second later, I'm catapulted forward over Liam's head and into the water. It's cold, but not as bad as I thought it would be. When I surface, giggling, I can taste the salt water on my lips.

"Told ya," Miles taunts. "Told ya no one can beat us!"

"Rematch," Liam says immediately. He turns and looks at me. "Sorry," he says. "You okay?"

"Yeah, I'm fine," I say. "It's actually kind of refreshing."

"We need a rematch," Liam says again.

"No way," Miles says, letting his fingertips skim the top

of the water. "You lost, fair and square."

"We did lose fair and square," Liam says. "That's why it's called a rematch."

"Why would I give you a chance to win when I'm undefeated?" Miles asks. Skye is still on his shoulders, and he spins her around. She squeals in delight. Does she like him? I hope not. He's so arrogant and jerky. He hasn't even acknowledged my presence once since I've been here, probably because I don't have fake boobs and/or a skimpy bikini. But that Skye is filled with surprises today, like how she outwitted me at my own game.

"Why would you not want to play again if you're so good?" Liam counters. "Unless you're scared."

"I'm not scared," Skye says, looking right at me. Her hands are resting under Miles's chin, and he opens his mouth and nibbles on her fingers. She squeals again.

"I'm not scared, either," I say, not wanting to be outdone.

"Okay," Miles agrees. "You're on."

I put my hands on Liam's shoulders so he can bend down and hoist me back up, but before he can, a voice calls to us from the shore.

"Liam! Aven!"

It's Izzy. She's standing on the shore, waving at us, her hair loose around her shoulders. She's changed into a pair of cutoff shorts and a black bandeau bikini top that shows off her toned arms.

"Oh," Liam says, sounding surprised. "It's Izzy."

"I thought she was with her dance team," I say, hoping I don't sound annoyed at the interruption. Even though I totally am.

"Come on," Miles demands. "Are you guys playing or not?"

"Just a second," Liam says, sounding impatient.

Izzy is wading into the ocean, the bottom of her denim cutoffs turning dark blue in the water. "Hey," she says, giving Liam a kiss on his lips. "Miss me?"

"Always," he says, and my heart breaks. It's the same way it breaks every time he says something like that to her, the kind of tiny little break that doesn't seem like much when it happens, but adds up to something big over time. It's like poking yourself over and over again, so lightly that you might not even feel it, until later when you realize you've given yourself a big bruise that aches and throbs through the night. That's how it feels when Izzy and Liam say something nice to each other, or kiss, or hold hands, or any of the thousands of other things you do when you're in a relationship with someone. It stings a tiny bit in the moment, so slight that I might not even feel it for more than a second. But all of these little moments add up to one big hurt that washes over me later, usually when I'm alone, usually at night, usually when I'm in my room and I have a chance to stop and breathe and think about my day.

"We're playing sword fight," I say. "Um, I mean, crab fight."

Izzy looks at me, standing there with Liam and Miles and Skye. Any other girl would probably think it was a little strange that her boyfriend had another girl up on his shoulders, playing a game that's actually kind of intimate. But not Izzy.

She just gives a half smile and leans into Liam. "Is that how you got all wet?" she asks me.

"Yes," I say, suddenly self-conscious about the fact that the three of them look like they could be in an ad for *Spring Break*, while my hair is dripping all over and I can tell my eyeliner is smudged.

"Are we playing or not?" Miles demands. "Let's go!"

"Um . . ." Liam looks back and forth between me and Izzy. I can tell he doesn't know what to do. So I do what I always do when Liam is forced to decide between me and Izzy—I make it easy for him.

"You guys should play," I say. "I need to get back to my room anyway. I just remembered I have to get something to Mr. Beals for the Student Action Committee." It's a lie, of course. There's nothing to give Mr. Beals for the Student Action Committee, and even if there was, it wouldn't be urgent.

"Are you sure?" Izzy asks. But she's already wrapping her arms around Liam, already climbing up his body gracefully.

They move together in synch, totally at ease with each other. It makes sense. Once you've had sex with someone, climbing onto their shoulders probably isn't that weird. But still. Isn't Izzy supposed to be mad at him because she thinks he's cheating on her?

"I'm sure," I say.

But they're not really paying attention to me anymore.

I walk back up the beach a ways to where I left my shorts and tank top. I pick them up and pull them on over my bathing suit, having to tug at them because putting dry clothes on over a wet bathing suit is kind of hard.

I turn around, mostly just to torture myself, and sure enough, they're already ensconced in their game. Izzy's laughing as she pushes at Skye, and I watch as Liam holds her tight and Izzy bites her lip in determination. A couple of pushes later, Skye falls into the water.

"You cheated!" Miles yells.

But Liam whoops and slides Izzy off his shoulders and into the water, then scoops her into his arms and kisses her on the lips in celebration.

I turn back around before I see anything else.

It's another sting, another tiny prick adding to the bigger wound. I ignore it as best I can, which isn't as hard as you would think. After all, I'm used to it.

I'm halfway to the hotel when my phone buzzes with that email again.

Before graduation, I will . . . *tell the truth*.

I have to. I have to tell him the truth.

Because all those little hurts, all those little heartbreaks, are starting to become too much to bear.

I'll do it the very next chance I get. No more waiting. No more wondering. Just doing.

FIVE

ON THE OTHER HAND, I DEFINITELY COULD just be having a weak moment. I mean, just because that email showed up on this trip doesn't mean I have to tell Liam while we're here. All the email says is before *graduation*. But there's still time before graduation—a couple of months. A couple of months is a long time. Sixty days. Eight weeks. That's a lot of hours. Math isn't my strong suit, otherwise I would figure it out.

The point is, there will be plenty of opportunities to tell him how I feel. Plenty of opportunities to make sure the moment is absolutely perfect. And yes, you would think there would be lots of perfect moments on this trip, since we're on an amazing vacation in an amazing place. But really, that's not always how it works. Just because something looks like the perfect moment on the outside doesn't mean it actually is.

It could be, like, masquerading as one. It's like a grand gesture. Girls always want guys to make some big, grand gesture for them—flowers, poems, fireworks, hot air balloon rides. But sometimes grand gestures aren't all they're cracked up to be. You don't know if the guy who's getting you flowers and acting like he loves you is going to be cheating on you the next week.

Which is why it might not be the best idea to tell Liam how I feel on this vacation. I have to wait for the right time, not get caught up in the heat of the moment. The real right time might be later. Much later. Like next week. Or next month.

Of course, Liam and I probably aren't going to be doing anything different over the next two months than we have been for the past four years. And if I didn't think any of *those* moments were the right time to tell him, then what makes me think that any of the moments coming up are going to be the right one?

Sigh. I keep walking down the beach, trying to distract myself from my thoughts, not quite sure what to do or where to go. I'm not really that excited to go back to the hotel. I mean, what would I even *do* back there? Sit in my room and feel sorry for myself? I have a couple of friends from the Student Action Committee I could text, but hanging out with them doesn't sound that appealing either.

So I just keep wandering until I come upon a tiny

outdoor bar high on the sand, closer to the parking lot than the ocean. It looks like a little tiki hut, with a straw roof and palm trees planted on each side. A bartender is making tropical-looking drinks and serving them to a young couple.

I'm suddenly aware of the sun beating down on me and the parched feeling in the back of my throat. I hesitate for a second, because obviously I'm not twenty-one, but there's a sign posted advertising virgin drinks, and there are a few kids my age sitting on the lime-green bar stools.

I take a seat in one of the middle chairs, and the bartender comes over immediately. He's a couple of years older than me, and he's wearing a tight black T-shirt that has *Siesta Key Beach Club* written in tiny white letters on one side. "Hi," he says, flashing me a smile. "What can I get you?"

"What do you recommend?" I ask.

"Hmm." He strokes his chin and pretends to be thinking about it. He looks me up and down, like I'm a puzzle that needs to be solved. "For you? A pineapple mango slush."

"Yum," I say, giving him a smile. "Sounds perfect."

I watch as he cuts up the pineapple and mango, then whirls everything together in a blender. He pours it into a fancy-looking glass, then sticks an orange-and-green umbrella into the drink and puts a slice of pineapple on the rim. He sets it in front of me with a flourish.

"That's it?" I ask, looking at the glass dubiously.

"What do you mean?"

"Nothing, I just . . . I mean, it's supposed to be tropical and special. But you just put some fruit in a blender and then poured it into a glass."

"I'm going to pretend you didn't say that," he says, shaking his head sadly, like I'm so naive he feels sorry for me. "Because I'm a nice guy. And after you have a sip of that drink, you're going to feel really stupid for questioning my methods."

I shrug and take a sip. The sweet tanginess of the fruit explodes on my tongue, cool and refreshing and perfect. I almost moan in pleasure, that's how good it is. "Wow," I say, "you're right. This is amazing."

He smiles. "I'm Colin."

"Aven."

"Nice to meet you."

"Nice to meet you, too." I take another sip of my drink and the tension starts to flow out of my body. This is nice, sitting here with a delicious fruity drink and making conversation with the cute bartender.

"Are you here on a school trip?" Colin asks.

"Yeah," I say. "Senior trip."

"College?"

"High school," I say, before realizing it might make me look ridiculously uncool to be in high school instead of college. Not that it really matters. It's not like I have to impress this guy—I don't even know him. In fact, the upside to being in love with Liam for so long is that other guys mean noth-ing to me. No one has even been on my radar.

Well.

That's not completely true.

There was this one time when Lyla tried to hook me up with her camp friend's brother, who went to another school. He looked really cute in his picture, and I got excited. It was during this little period of time where I'd decided to get over Liam and I was doing all these things to work on myself, like trying to get interested in other guys and getting involved in self-esteem-boosting activities. I even started training for a marathon, which was actually great at first, because it got me into crazy good shape and my endorphins were through the roof.

But the camp friend's brother turned out to be not as cute as his picture and everything I saw on my long week-end runs made me think of Liam, so the whole thing just didn't really take. Lyla was disappointed, I think. Especially because she had to explain to her friend why it wasn't going to work out. Well, not explain as much as make up a lie. Obviously she wasn't going to tell her friend that her brother wasn't as cute in person as he was in his picture That would have been humiliating and mean. Besides, it wasn't really about how he looked in real life—he was fine. We just didn't have a connection.

"That's cool," Colin says, seemingly unfazed by the fact

that I'm in high school. "I'm a freshman at USF."

"Cool," I say. "I'm going to Northeastern."

"Nice." He grins at me. "So how long are you here for?"

"Just a few days." I take another small sip of my drink. It's so good and I'm so thirsty it's hard not to drink it down in big gulps, but I don't want to seem like a pig. "Our school couldn't afford for us to come for a whole week."

"You didn't have to do stupid fund-raisers to try to raise money?"

"Oh, we did," I say. "But we hardly raised anything." I grin, and he grins back at me.

"Well, a few days is better than nothing."

"Definitely."

My phone buzzes and I look down, hoping for a text from Izzy or Liam, letting me know they're done playing stupid crab fight and asking me where I am. But it's just that stupid email again.

Before graduation, I will . . . *tell the truth.*

La, la, la, not thinking about that.

"So what are you doing sitting here all by yourself?" Colin asks. He pulls a coconut out from behind the bar and starts cutting it, the knife slicing through the skin of the fruit perfectly on the first try.

"What are *you* doing here by yourself?" I counter. "They really let you use that knife unsupervised?"

"Yup," he says. "All you need is to be eighteen and take

a training class." He lowers his voice. "Of course, that's how my friend Frank came to be called Four-Finger Frank."

"Really?" I ask, horrified. "That's awful."

"No." He shakes his head. "I'm kidding."

"Oh." I laugh and take another sip of my slush. I'm feeling very relaxed, just sitting here chatting and drinking this refreshing tropical drink. Who says I have to do something big like tell Liam I'm in love with him? What is love, anyway? I mean, how do I know what it even *feels* like? Can you even love someone you've never had a romantic relationship with? I really doubt it. And when you think about it that way, it's all settled. I don't love Liam. I'm just in lust with him.

Of course, four years is a long time to just be in lust with someone. But it could happen. And you can't just go flying off the rails, telling someone you're in lust with them. Like, when your fourteen-year-old self sends you a crazy email talking about how you need to tell the truth before graduation, it has nothing to do with telling someone you're in lust with them. I mean, how stupid.

Besides, telling the truth is so ambiguous. And honestly, I don't even really remember what I meant exactly when I wrote that email. Yeah, I always *thought* it was about Liam, but how can I really know? Your brain can play tricks on you, especially after four years. It's like how eyewitnesses remember things that didn't even happen. It's not that they're lying, it's just that their brains get all confused. So even though I remember standing on that beach with Lyla and Quinn that day and thinking about Liam and making a promise to myself that I would tell him how I felt, that doesn't mean that's what really happened. I could have been talking about a million different things.

Ahhh. I feel a lot better now that I've finally made the decision that the stupid email means nothing.

"So what are you doing while you're here?" Colin asks. "Any big plans?"

"Oh," I say. "Um . . ." Somehow *I was going to tell my best friend I'm in love with him even though he has a girlfriend, but I just convinced myself not to a second ago* doesn't seem like it would be all that impressive.

"Bartender!" a girl calls from across the bar. She holds up her empty glass and clinks the ice.

"Be right back," Colin says, and then he winks at me.

He winked at me! A guy has never winked at me before. It seems kind of . . . flirty. Unless he winks at everyone. Or maybe it's a nervous tic. Although he doesn't seem like the kind of guy who has nervous tics. He's too good-looking, and besides, he was handling that coconut with a lot of confidence.

Was he . . . was he going to ask me out? Is that why he was asking what my plans were while I'm here? No. That doesn't make any sense. That kind of thing doesn't happen to me. I mean, he must meet tons of girls. He's a bartender in the middle of the beach. A hot one. Of all the girls he meets on a daily basis, why would he want to go out with me?

Unless he's—

My phone buzzes again, and I look down, ready to send that email right to the trash for what feels like the millionth time.

But it's not the stupid email.

It's Izzy.

Calling me.

She never calls me. She doesn't like talking on the phone. She's a text-only kind of girl. I hit answer. "Izzy?"

"Aven!" Her voice sounds panicked, and my heart slides up into my throat. Why does she sound so panicked? Has something happened? She was fine just a few minutes ago, splashing around in the ocean, happy as a clam. Or crab. Ha-ha. Has she found out about me and Liam, my plan to tell him how I feel?

"Izzy, what's wrong?"

"Aven," she says again. "I did something really bad."

"Oh." I let out a sigh of relief. If she did something really bad, then it can't have anything to do with me and Liam. That's one of the hazards of being friends with the girl-friend of the boy you're in love with—you're always afraid she's going to find out how you really feel. Wait. Did I say love? I meant lust. The boy you're in lust with.

"What did you do?" I ask, dragging my straw through my almost-empty glass.

"I did it," she says ominously. "I said I wasn't going to, I promised myself I wasn't going to, but I did. I did it! I couldn't stop myself!" Her voice is getting louder as she talks, until she's almost shrieking. She sounds a bit hysterical, honestly.

"Okay," I say. "Um, well, what was it?"

"Where are you?" she demands.

"I'm just sitting at this bar, having a drink," I say, the words sounding very grown-up and exciting. Just sitting at the bar having a drink and possibly flirting with the hot bartender, la, la, la.

"Which bar?" Izzy wants to know. "I'm coming there."

"It's on the beach," I say, "a little farther down from where we just were. Aren't you in the water with Liam?" I swivel around in my seat and shade my eyes from the sun, trying to see if I can spot her. You'd think it would be impossible, what with all the people, but after a second I actually see her, walking crookedly down the shore.

"No, I left," she says.

"I see you," I tell her. I stand up and wave my arms up in the air like a crazy person.

"See you in a second." The line goes dead.

A minute or two later, Izzy slides into the seat next to me. She looks slightly disheveled—her hair is sort of messed up, and the strap on the top of her bandeau top is askew.

She looks at my drink. "What is that?" she asks.

"Oh, a mango pineapple something," I say, taking

another sip and hoping she doesn't ask me to share. "It's really good. You should get one."

"Is there any alcohol in it?"

I shake my head, and she looks vaguely disappointed.

"So what happened?" I ask.

She opens her mouth to answer me, but then her face crumples and she bursts into tears.

"Oh my God," I say. "Izzy! What happened?" I reach out and put my arms around her, pulling her toward me. But she's crying too hard to answer. "Tell me what happened," I soothe. "I'm sure whatever it is, it isn't that bad."

She pulls back and wipes her eyes with one of the tiny square napkins that's sitting on the bar. She whispers something so quietly that I can't understand what she's saying.

"What?" I prompt. "I can't hear you."

"I looked in his phone," she says. "Liam's. I looked in it."

"Oh, Izzy," I breathe. "Why did you do that?"

"I feel horrible!" she says. "I know! But I couldn't help it! He was in the water and we were playing that dumb game, you know, with the sword fighting or whatever, and then I knocked Skye off Miles, and Miles got really mad and went off to find a new partner, because he said Skye was the weak link—"

"Wow, what an asshole," I say, but Izzy just keeps going.

"So then Liam said he was going to run to the bathroom, and I was lying on the beach, and I was thinking about how happy I was, and how perfect everything was, you know, to just be here in this amazing place on this amazing trip with this amazing boy. And I told myself there was no way he was cheating on me, that Liam doesn't do things like that." She's out of breath from talking so fast, and she stops for a second.

I take the last sip of my drink and wait for her to finish.

"So then I saw his phone sitting there in the sand where he left it. And I could see him walking down the beach, toward the pavilion, and I thought, if I can just look in his phone and see for myself, if I can just look and make *sure* that he's not talking to anyone else, then the moment really *will* be perfect, you know?"

I want to tell her that if she felt the need to *make* the moment perfect, then it probably wasn't all that perfect to begin with, but I know it's definitely not the right time for reality. She doesn't need to hear *reason*. She needs support.

"Okay," I say slowly.

"So I looked in his phone. I did it. I picked his phone right up and just started going through it, like it was nothing. And there were calls. A few of them. Missed ones. From someone named Annabelle."

Annabelle. I don't know anyone named Annabelle in our class. Maybe she's a junior? Or a sophomore? But if Liam is cheating on Izzy with some girl named Annabelle, wouldn't I have heard him at least mention it? And since when is Liam making tons of phone calls anyway? He's a guy. He texts, and even then it's sporadic.

"Were there any texts?" I ask nonchalantly. I swirl the paper umbrella around in my empty glass and hope Izzy thinks I'm asking because I'm worried about her and not for my own curiosity.

Annabelle, Annabelle, Annabelle. Her name sounds cute, like the kind of girl who wears quirky outfits and has a quirky hairstyle to match. The kind of girl who has pigtails and cute freckles and lives a somewhat sheltered life. Liam probably has to teach her things. Like how to eat a lobster and change a tire. And sexual things. Maybe he's so busy teaching her sexual things that he hasn't had any time or energy left over to have sex with Izzy.

"There was just one," she says. "From Annabelle to Liam. All it said was 'call me tonight at eight.'" She narrows her eyes, then reaches over and grabs my drink, taking a long, slurpy sip, apparently not even noticing the glass is empty. "Obviously he deleted the rest of them. Just in case." She starts chewing on the straw, her teeth working furiously.

"Well, let's not jump to conclusions," I say. "Maybe it was something totally innocent." But even as I'm saying it, I know it's not true. Come on. Something totally innocent with a girl named Annabelle who Izzy and I know nothing about? Liam wouldn't hide it from us if it was aboveboard.

Annabelle. Annabelle. Annabelle. Her name starts reverberating in my head, like when you start saying a word over and over until it starts sounding weird. She's very murky and threatening, this Annabelle. With Izzy, I know exactly what I'm getting. Annabelle's a total blank. She could look like anything, be like anything, sound like anything.

"Ha!" Izzy says. "There's no way it's something innocent." She's lost the controlled look she had on her face before, and she's back to looking a little wild. She picks up my glass and pounds it on the bar. "Can we get some more drinks over here?" she yells to Colin.

He turns from where he's serving a couple of piña coladas to a twentysomething couple.

"You have a friend," he says when he's back over on our side of the bar.

"Yeah," I say. "This is Izzy. Izzy, this is Colin."

"You two know each other?" she asks.

"Oh, yeah, we go way back," Colin says, flashing me a smile.

"He's kidding," I say. "We just met."

"Oh." Izzy looks interested. "Well, we need a couple more drinks."

"Sure," he says. "You want the same as before?"

"Yes, please," I say, not being able to comprehend the fact that something could be better than the drink I just had. "Two this time."

"You got it." He turns around and gets to work cutting fruit.

"He was totally flirting with you," Izzy whispers once he's out of earshot.

"No, he wasn't," I say. But I can feel my face get hot. "He's just a bartender. He talks to everyone like that. He has to work for his tips."

Izzy shakes her head. "He was looking at you in a certain way," she says. "He wasn't just being friendly."

"How do you know?"

"Because I know things." She shrugs. It's true. Izzy is one of those people who somehow kind of just *know* things. "You should flirt back," Izzy says. "You need to have some fun. You haven't dated anyone in a while."

"I just haven't met anyone I like," I say quickly.

"Well, you should like *him*," Izzy says. "He's seriously sexy."

"He also lives in Florida."

"Well, that's perfect," Izzy says. "You can have a passionate vacation fling with him." She sighs. "Relationships aren't all they're cracked up to be, Aven. Take it from me."

"Oh, Iz," I say. "I'm sure it's going to be fine. I think you should just ask him about it."

"I can't!" she says. "He'll know I looked in his phone."

"Well, would that be the worst thing in the world? You could just say you were feeling weird and you're really sorry, but you looked in his phone and you saw something that made you concerned."

Izzy's blue eyes widen into saucers, and she looks at me like I'm crazy. "Are you *mad*?" she asks. "I can't just go and tell Liam that I looked in his phone. I'll seem crazy."

I want to point out that she *did* look in his phone and maybe she *is* being a little crazy, but obviously that wouldn't be helpful.

Colin returns then and sets our drinks down in front of us. "There you go," he says. "Two drinks for two beautiful ladies."

"Thanks," Izzy says distractedly, like she's used to getting called beautiful.

"Thanks," I say, sliding my drink closer to me.

"So listen," he says, "what are you guys doing tomorrow night?" He says "you guys," but he's looking at me.

"I have plans," Izzy says quickly. "But Aven's free."

I am? She does?

"Cool," Colin says. "Well, if you want, a bunch of us are going on this sunset cruise." He picks my phone up from where I've set it on the bar and calls himself so I'll have his number in my call history. "Text me, and I'll give you the info."

He winks at me again, and then disappears to the other side of the bar, where the twentysomething couple starts asking him something about their drinks.

"Oh my God," Izzy says. "He wants to take you on a date."

"No, he doesn't," I say. But maybe he does. I mean, what's so weird about that? I'm kind of cute and very charming, and people have told me I'm really good at witty banter.

"Yeah, he does. And you should go. You need to have some fun in your life." She sighs. "Not like me. I have problems." She grabs my arm again, like she did earlier when we were in the bathroom at the airport. "You need to find out about this Annabelle for me, Aven. Liam will tell you. He tells you everything."

"Obviously not," I say. "Since he hasn't told me about her yet."

"Yeah, but he *will*. You just have to ask him."

"Oh, okay. I'll just be like, 'Hey, Liam, do you know anyone named Annabelle? Just you know, out of curiosity.'"

"You could tell him you looked in his phone," Izzy says slowly.

"Izzy!" I say, shocked that she would even suggest such a thing. "But I didn't."

"No, I know," she says, waving her hand like it was a joke, even though I think she was half hoping I'd go for it. "I was just kidding." She takes in a deep breath, and then she starts crying again. "I just can't believe he might be cheating on me," she says. "I mean, I knew things were a little weird between us, but I never—I didn't—I didn't think he WOULD DO THAT!"

"Okay, okay," I say, putting my arm around her. "I'll try

to figure out a way to ask him."

"You will?" she asks, sniffling.

I pick another napkin up off the bar and hand it to her. She blows her nose loudly. "Yes," I say. "I'll try to figure out a way."

"Thanks, Aven," Izzy says. "You're a really good friend."

Yeah.

A really good friend.

A really good friend who's in love with your boyfriend.

SIX

OKAY.

This doesn't have to be that hard.

Izzy was right when she said that Liam tells me everything. Or at least, he usually does. So all I have to do is ask him some leading questions about what's happening in his life, and hope that maybe he'll bring up this whole Annabelle thing on his own. I mean, I don't have to come straight out and ask if he's cheating. I'm sure there are a million different ways to get it out of him. I'll just use my witty banter.

Of course, first I have to get him alone.

And Liam has other ideas.

He calls me later that afternoon, just as I'm finishing a long shower in which I was attempting to wash the salt water out of my hair and the sand off my body. I never knew how much sand could end up all over you after some time at the beach. It's really a miracle that any of it even *stays* on the beach, what with the way it just *clings* to people. Unless I'm some kind of sand magnet. Or sand trap. (Get it? Witty banter, ha-ha.)

"Where have you been?" Liam asks when I answer. "I've been texting you."

"Sorry, I was in the shower," I say. I've wrapped myself in a towel, but my hair is still soaking wet, and it's dripping all over the bathroom floor. Something tells me Lyla and Quinn aren't going to be too happy about me messing up the common areas. I grab another towel off the rack that's hanging on the wall and drop it on the floor. I push it around with my foot, trying to mop up the water.

Hmm. The towel is getting kind of soaked. And dirty. I wonder what Quinn and Lyla would be madder about—the floor being wet, or me using up all the towels. We can probably get more from housekeeping, but still. Hopefully I won't be here when they come back and realize what I've done to the bathroom.

"Oh," Liam says. "Nice mental picture."

"Whatever," I say automatically, the way I do whenever Liam says something that could be construed as flirting.

"Anyway, what are you doing tonight?" he asks. "Juliana Peters is having a party in her room."

"Juliana?" I say warily. I don't know much about her, except that she talks in the third person and is always screaming in the halls at school, like moving between rooms is something to get worked up about.

"Yeah, I know," Liam says. "But there's going to be beer. And then afterward we can meet up with Izzy and her dance team. They're going to walk the beach at midnight."

"I don't know," I say slowly. "I mean, isn't that something you and Izzy might want to do alone?" Talk about being a third wheel.

"No," he says. "Her whole team is going to be there, looking for constellations. Ten giggling girls looking at stars sounds like a particularly horrible kind of torture, but Izzy really wants me there." He pauses, and I don't say anything.

Obviously the only reason Izzy wants Liam there is so she can make sure he's not with someone else. But then why doesn't Izzy just cancel her stupid midnight walk with her dance team and spend time with Liam? And why is Liam inviting me anyway? Is he trying to use me so that whenever he's around Izzy, he can tell Annabelle I was there, too, like some kind of insurance policy?

It's annoying the way they both might be using me for personal gain. Or relationship gain. Whatever you want to call it, it's irritating. Why should I have to be a part of their secrets and lies?

"I'll go to the party," I say. "But I don't feel like doing the beach walk."

"Why not?"

"I dunno," I say. "It just doesn't sound that fun."

"Are you kidding? It's going to be so fun. We can take

pictures and then later I can force you to read some stupid book about astronomy. Or even better, a novel with a main character who's an astronomer from the nineteenth century or something."

"You just said it was going to be torture."

"No, I said if you left me alone with ten girls it was going to be torture."

"Sorry," I say. "But I actually have plans with, ah, Gabby Ronson. You know, from the Student Action Committee?"

"At midnight?"

"Yeah," I say. "At midnight."

There's a pause, like maybe Liam wants to say something else. But he must change his mind, because a second later, he says, "Okay. So I'll just see you at the party then?"

"Sure," I say. "Just text me the room number and time."

"Done."

The thing about high school parties is that if you've been to one, you've pretty much been to them all. There's always a bunch of guys doing something ridiculous, like getting crazy drunk and peeing in someone's refrigerator, or stealing someone's parents' checkbook, or going outside and throwing people's lawn chairs into the pool.

Everyone's drinking cheap beer, because we usually have to pay someone to buy it for us. It's either that or steal it from our parents, and if we do that, we can't take anything good because then they'll end up noticing it's gone.

When I say "we," I really mean "they," because even though I've been to more parties than I can count, I don't really drink. I don't get the point of it, really. You drink a lot and then you just end up feeling sick and like you want to throw up? I get the idea of wanting to have a good buzz, get stuck right in that place where you feel woozy and happy and relaxed. But no one at these parties ever stops there. They can't, because you never know when a party is going to get broken up.

It's actually pretty pathetic, really, when you think about it.

The sad thing is, I'm not sure college is going to be any better. At least from what I've seen in the movies.

When I get to Juliana's room, it takes my eyes a second to adjust to the darkness. The sun has gone down, and apparently no one's thought to turn on any lights.

Juliana is twirling around in the middle of the room, a beer in her hand. She doesn't look like she's at all worried about getting caught partying in her room. In fact, she looks happy and relaxed. She's probably going to be sick later. Oh, well. I've never been friends with Juliana, so not my problem.

I spot Liam over in the corner, by the little kitchenette, talking with Jeff Hearne. I hesitate, not sure exactly what to do. I don't really know Jeff that well, and so it feels weird to just walk up and intrude on their conversation.

But I don't have to worry about it for long, because Liam

meets my eye across the room and motions me over. When I get to him, Jeff wanders off, muttering something about how there are no hot girls at this party. I'm not sure if I should be insulted or not, since he hardly even looked at me, but whatever.

"Hey," Liam says, his face lighting up into a smile. He's wearing a pair of baggy jeans and a red long-sleeved shirt. His hair is damp, like he just got out of the shower. He smells like soap and a touch of cologne and his face is tan from the beach and I can see a tiny place on the side of his neck where he nicked himself shaving and he looks so hot I can hardly take it.

"Hi," I say.

"You want something to drink?"

"Is there soda?"

He picks one up from the table next to him and hands it to me. "I snagged it for you."

"Thanks," I say, popping the top and taking a sip.

"This party is lame," Liam says, looking around.

"Well, it's stupid to have a party in a hotel room," I say. "We're at the beach. We should be partying outside."

"Yeah, but you can't drink outside," Liam points out.

"Which is why this whole party is a joke. I can't believe people would rather stay inside just to get drunk instead of being outside in the fresh air."

"Yeah." Liam takes a sip of his drink, and I realize he's drinking Sprite. Not that Liam's a huge drinker, but he'll usually have a beer or two, especially since he knows I'm always willing to drive him home.

"You're not drinking?" I ask.

"Nah." He swallows, and his Adam's apple bobs up and down. He doesn't offer any other information, which is weird.

"How come?" I ask.

"Just don't feel like it." Hmmm. Is he not drinking because he's afraid he's going to get a little sloppy and let something slip about Annabelle to Izzy? Maybe this is my opening! Maybe I can push Liam a little about why he's not drinking, get him to admit something.

"Why not?" I ask.

"I just don't." He sounds slightly annoyed. "What's the big deal?"

"It's not a big deal," I say. "It's just that you usually have a beer, so I just figured you'd have one tonight. You know, since it's vacation and all."

"Yeah, well, people are doing a lot of things they don't usually do just because it's vacation."

I frown. The statement is confusing—it's like a double negative or something. Is he trying to say people aren't being themselves on vacation because he's trying to justify the fact that he's not drinking? Maybe he's just looking for a way to start confiding in me about Annabelle. Maybe he's not worried about making sense because he just wants an opening.

"What do you mean?" I ask gently.

"Nothing." He shrugs and takes another sip of his Sprite. "Just that you're doing things you wouldn't normally do, either."

"Me?"

"Yeah."

"Like what?" This is shocking. I haven't done anything I wouldn't normally do since, like, fifth grade.

"Nothing," he says. "Just forget it."

"No, I don't want to forget it," I say. "What are you talking about?"

"It's not a big deal."

"Well, obviously it is, if you brought it up."

"It's just that you usually aren't the type to hook up with random guys."

"Random guys? What are you taking about?" I look down at the Sprite in his hand, wondering if maybe someone spiked it with something. I wish I had that new nail polish, the one that lets you see if someone's slipped a drug into your drink. You dip your finger in and if your nail turns dark, it means your drink was spiked. If I was wearing it, I'd dip it right into Liam's Sprite, no questions asked.

"That guy you met today on the beach. The bartender."

"Oh." I swallow. "How did you know about that?"

"Izzy told me."

"Oh," I say again. "What did she tell you?"

"Just that you were flirting with some tool on the beach and you gave him your number and you guys are going out tomorrow night. Which, by the way, was supposed to be the night we went to Discovery Cove, but whatever."

"I thought we weren't going to Discovery Cove because of the way they treat the dolphins."

"We're not."

"Okay."

Liam seems agitated. He's gazing out across the party, not even really looking at me. He tilts his head to the side and taps his foot to the music that's coming from the speakers in the corner.

"Are you . . . I mean, are you mad at me about something?"

"No. It's just weird that you wouldn't have mentioned meeting some guy on the beach, that's all."

"It just happened," I say. "Like, two hours ago. And there was nothing to really tell. I met a guy, he asked for my number."

"What kind of guy invites a girl he doesn't know on a cruise? It sounds shady, Aven, and I don't like it."

"You don't even know him," I say. But then I stop and shake my head. This conversation is getting out of control, and honestly, there's no reason for it. It's a dumb thing to fight about. Liam's just worried about me, which is totally understandable. And besides, who knows what Izzy told Liam about Colin? She probably made it out like he was some sex-crazed maniac inviting me back to his drug lair or something.

"You're defending some guy you just met?" Liam asks.

"What? No. I'm not defending anyone." I take a deep breath. "Look, he's just some guy I met on the beach. I'm sorry I didn't mention it, but I didn't think it was important. And you know I would never do anything stupid, Liam. I would never put myself in a situation where I might be in danger, and honestly, it's a little insulting that you think I would."

Liam finally turns to look at me, and for a second, no, not even a second, maybe a half a second, I feel like I see something flash in his eyes, something I've never seen before.

Jealousy.

But that's crazy. Could Liam really be jealous of me and another guy?

But then it's gone, and his face softens and he's back to being the Liam I know, the strong and steady friend who's always been there for me.

"You're right," he says. "I'm sorry. I shouldn't have given you a hard time. I was just worried about you, and I didn't like that you didn't tell me. It felt weird, like you were hiding something."

"I wasn't hiding anything," I say. "It was a nonissue. Honestly, it didn't even register as something worth mentioning."

"But are you going out on the boat with him?"

"I don't know."

"So you're considering it." He sounds annoyed, which

makes *me* annoyed. Why are we even fighting about this? Who cares if some guy asked me to go on a cruise with him?

"Why are we fighting about this?" I ask, and I can hear the annoyance in my voice now, which pisses me off because I can't believe I'm getting worked up over something so stupid.

"Because you didn't tell me that some sleaze was hitting on you, and I don't like it."

"He wasn't sleazy!"

"Now you're defending him again?"

"You know what," I say, really worked up now, "I can't believe we're even having this conversation. Especially when you don't feel the need to tell me things, either."

"What?"

"You heard me. You keep things from me, too, Liam, and I don't give you this kind of shit about it."

"What do I keep from you?" he asks. His voice is measured, like he's trying hard to keep this from blowing up into a huge thing, but it's also guarded, like he's afraid I might have found something out. Which I have. But to admit that wouldn't be fair to Izzy, because then I'd have to explain exactly how I know about Annabelle.

"Nothing," I say, shaking my head. "Just forget it."

"Sure," he says. "Let's just forget it."

"Fine."

"Fine."

We stand there for a minute or two, not saying anything, just watching the people at the party. And then I start thinking about how I only came to this stupid party because Liam wanted me to and how he has some secret girl on the side that he's not even telling me about.

So I put my soda down on the table and say, "You know what? I'm not feeling that great. I think I'm going to go."

I want him to ask me what's wrong, I want him to tell me not to go, or that the party is lame and he'll leave with me, but he doesn't say any of that. Instead he just shrugs and says, "Okay."

I'm halfway to the door when I think about turning back and telling him I'm sorry. I have no reason to really be upset with him—it's a stupid misunderstanding, and whatever he has going on with this Annabelle girl honestly has nothing to do with me. It's between him and Izzy. He's not my boyfriend, he never has been, and if he wants to cheat on his girlfriend and not tell me about it, then that's his business.

But I don't turn around.

Instead, I just keep walking.

Once I'm in the hallway, I realize I have nothing to do for the rest of the night. Izzy's with her dance team, and obviously Liam's back at the party. I wonder what he's going to do now that I left. Maybe he'll hang out with his stupid jock friends. Or maybe he'll call Annabelle.

Whatever.

Not my problem.

I think about just heading back to my room, but something about that seems like a cop-out—if I just end up back in my room, I've let Liam win. Why should I give him the power to ruin my night just because he felt like picking a fight?

So I text Reva Tannenbaum, this girl I know from the Student Action Committee. She texts me back right away, letting me know that she and a couple of her friends are at an outdoor restaurant on Ocean Boulevard.

So I head down there for a couple of hours, making small talk with people I don't know that well and trying not to think about Liam. I eat nachos and drink fruity drinks and have more ice cream and buy a tiny key chain that looks like a Florida license plate and has my name on it, because you can get them custom-made and they never have my name on anything.

By the time I get back to my room, I'm feeling a little better. My stomach is pleasantly full, I'm drunk on the ocean air, and even though I'm not close with Reva and her friends, they were still nice and fun to hang out with.

I open the door to my room slowly, not sure if Quinn and Lyla are going to be there. Quinn's bed is empty, but

Lyla's sleeping in hers, and so is her boyfriend, Derrick.

Wow. How totally disrespectful. She didn't even *ask* us if it was okay to have a guest spend the night, much less a *male* guest. They probably had sex in that bed. How disgusting.

And what happened to the school rule about coed sleepovers? It was one of the main points in the informational packet that got handed out. In fact, I thought Mr. Beals was supposed to be checking everyone's rooms at night. Wow. This trip is totally mismanaged—people drinking in hotel rooms, people having sex in hotel rooms. Our parents definitely wouldn't be happy if they knew what we were getting up to.

Thank God Lyla and Derrick are already sleeping. The last thing I want to do is make small talk with those two. I change quickly into my pajamas and then slide into bed. The cot is actually surprisingly comfortable. Either that or I'm just exhausted, because it actually feels cozy in here, with the doors to the balcony open and the breeze sliding in. I can smell the freshness of the ocean air, and if I listen hard enough, I can hear the waves sliding onto the shore.

My phone buzzes from where I've set it down on the floor next to me. My heart leaps. *Liam.* It has to be. Texting me to tell me he's sorry, that he can't believe we got into a fight over something so ridiculous.

But it's not Liam.

It's that stupid email.

Before graduation, I will . . . *tell the truth.*

Thank God I didn't listen to it.

Thank God I didn't tell Liam how I felt.

I delete the email and set my phone back on the floor.

The thought flits through my head that maybe I'm using this thing with Liam, this thing with Annabelle and our fight, as an excuse to not tell him how I feel.

But then I decide that's not true. People don't stay friends for four years if there's something more there. If Liam had wanted to be more than friends, he would have asked me out, he would have made a move. There have been hundreds of times he could have tried to kiss me, or tell me how he felt, or given me some kind of sign.

When Izzy moved here last year, he didn't become friends with her and spend a bunch of time getting to know her. He decided he liked her, and he asked her out after, like, two days.

Two days to ask out Izzy.

Four years of being friends with me, talking to me every day, without giving me any indication that he likes me as more than a friend.

It's time for me to really face the truth.

Liam and I are just friends.

And the sooner I accept that, the better.

SEVEN

THE NEXT MORNING, I'M WOKEN UP BY A knock on our hotel room door.

Probably Liam.

But I'm not answering it.

He can stay out there for all I care.

I roll over and squeeze my eyes shut tight. I even put my thumb in my mouth. I know it's lame, but I've done it ever since I was a baby. I tried for a while to break the habit, but I can't. I've gotten to the point where I don't need to do it every night, but it still helps if I'm stressed or having trouble sleeping.

The knocking stops. Wow. Talk about giving up easily. Humph. Maybe he just went down the hall so he could call my phone and try to wake me up. I wonder what I'll do if he *does* call me. Will I answer it? I'll probably have to. It could wake everyone else up and then—

"Lyla!" comes a loud whisper from the other side of the door.

Lyla? Why would Liam be calling for *Lyla*? Does he think he can try to get her to talk to me about how ridiculous I'm being? Why would he do that? He knows Lyla and I aren't friends anymore.

"Lyla!" comes the voice again.

It's a little louder this time, loud enough for me to realize it's not Liam out there after all. It's some other guy. Some other guy calling for Lyla when she's in bed with her boyfriend! How totally scandalous. This is definitely not something I want to get involved in, so I keep my eyes shut tight. A few seconds later, I hear Lyla getting out of bed and opening the door.

"Finally," the mystery boy says. He doesn't sound mad, though. He sounds cocky, like he knew she would come no matter how long it took.

I crack my eyes a little bit and try to see who it is. But the open door is blocking my view.

Then the boy says, "Rough night?" His voice has a sexy lilt to it, almost like he's teasing her. Which is pretty messed up, if you ask me. I mean, Lyla has a boyfriend. A boyfriend who's *sleeping in her bed*.

"No." Lyla says. She sounds mad, like she can't believe this guy has the nerve to wake her up. But I notice she doesn't ask what he's doing here or seem all that surprised. Is Lyla cheating on Derrick? Whenever I see them in the halls at school, they seem happy. And again, *he's in her bed*. She had *sex* with him last night, and now she's got some other guy after her. Why is it that Lyla has two guys and I have none?

I listen as the guy at the door asks Lyla to go get coffee with him.

She sounds annoyed and tells him no, but I know Lyla well enough to tell that she's not really *that* annoyed. She has that tone in her voice she gets when she's trying to act like she's mad, but deep down she wants you to convince her to do whatever it is you're asking her to do.

Then she steps out into the hall, and I can't hear the rest of what she's saying, because her voice is all muffled. A few moments later, she comes back into the room, and I hear her rustling around before she leaves again. Only this time, she doesn't come back.

Great. Lyla's taken off with some guy and left me alone with Derrick. Where the hell is Quinn, anyway? Her bed is still empty, and it doesn't look like she slept in it last night. What if Derrick wakes up and wants to know where Lyla went? I'm a horrible liar. My lip starts twitching and I talk really fast and add unnecessary details to the lie that make it completely obvious I'm not telling the truth.

I'm tempted to just leave the room, but I have nowhere to go. I haven't heard from Liam since our fight, and Izzy . . . Actually, where *is* Izzy? I haven't heard from her, either. Are they both mad at me now? Did Liam somehow convince Izzy that since he's mad at me, she should be, too?

I toss and turn for another hour or so, before finally sending her a text.

What's up? How was your night?

Once she replies, I'll tell her about the fight I had with Liam. Maybe she talked to him about it and she has some insights. Maybe he told her it was totally ridiculous, the way we fought. Maybe she told him he shouldn't be so mean to me, that the guy I was flirting with wasn't a douche, that I hardly even liked him, that if I didn't mention it, then it obviously wasn't that big of a deal.

Unless.

Unless she went the other way, and told Liam that Colin was hot and cool and cutting mangos and looking sexy while doing it. Maybe Izzy said she couldn't figure out why I wasn't interested in him, and then maybe Liam and Izzy put two and two together and realized it was because I was in love with Liam! And now they're both not talking to me until they can figure out how to handle the situation.

Of course, that scenario is highly unlikely, since Izzy's probably still upset about the whole Annabelle debacle. But maybe they worked that out, too. Maybe Annabelle's, like, Liam's cousin or something, and it was all a big misunderstanding.

Maybe they even talked about their boring sex life, and

Liam said of course he wanted to sleep with Izzy, that he was just nervous about her thinking that's all he wanted when their connection obviously goes so much deeper. And then Izzy said of course she didn't think that, and then the two of them spent all night having sex in a bunch of different places. On the beach. In their rooms. In . . . I don't know, other romantic places people go to have sex. Like a hot tub or something. Not that there are any hot tubs in this hotel, at least that I've seen, but I'll bet there's a pool and a—

Oh.

Text from Izzy.

My night was horrible!!!! Can you meet for bfast?

I text her back.

Yes. Where?

Cute café on Ocean Boulevard.

She texts me the address.

Okay. Give me 30 mins? I want to grab a quick shower.

Okay.

I hesitate with my hand over my phone, wondering if I should ask her for more details, so I know what I'm getting myself into. Did she and Liam have a fight about Annabelle? Did they break up? Whose side am I on?

Obviously I'm closer friends with Liam. But Liam shouldn't have cheated on Izzy (if he did), *and* he shouldn't have been so mean to me last night. But Izzy shouldn't have looked in his phone—if she had an issue with their relationship, she should have just asked him about it.

Whatever. I can't start driving myself crazy with all the what-ifs. So I push them out of my mind and head for the shower.

Twenty minutes later, I'm clean and dressed and ready to go meet Izzy. I'm over by my bed, sliding some sunglasses into my bag and trying not to wake Derrick, when the hotel room door opens.

Lyla. She's back.

Panic flows through me, and I quickly sit down on my cot. I don't know why. It's like I want her to think I've been sleeping this whole time or something, even though I'm dressed. Not that it matters, because Lyla looks completely oblivious to everything going on around her. She blinks fast, like she's trying to hold back tears, but her face is blank and emotionless.

"What's wrong?" I blurt, before I can help myself. The last thing I want is to get involved in Lyla's drama. Okay, fine, that's not completely true. I mean, I do miss her.

She turns to look at me, like she's surprised I'm even in the room.

"Nothing's wrong," she says.

Liar. "You're getting that look on your face," I say.

"What look?"

"The look you always get when you're about to cry."

"I do not have that look on my face!" She thinks about

it. "And besides, I don't get a look on my face when I'm about to cry."

"Yes, you do," I say. "Your bottom lip gets all wobbly and you get these weird little wrinkles at the side of your eyes." She tilts her head, considering, and her crying look goes away for a second. So I try to make a joke. "If you're going to cry, you should probably just cry, because if you keep letting your face get wrinkled like that, you're probably going to need Botox when you're older."

She bursts into tears.

"Oh, wow," I say, feeling horrible. "Lyla, I'm sorry. I was just kidding. You're not going to need Botox when you're older. You have really nice skin."

"I'm not crying because of that," she says. "I just . . ." She trails off and takes in a shuddering breath, like she's trying to figure out exactly what it is she wants to say, but then her eyes fall on Derrick, sprawled out under the covers on her bed.

She looks at me again and opens her mouth to say something. I wait expectantly, but instead of explaining, she turns and runs out of the room! Great. Now what am I supposed to do? I wait a second to see if she comes back, but she doesn't. So I follow her. She might not want anything to do with me, but *I* want something to do with her, and besides, she's obviously upset. It would be mean not to at least check on her.

When I get out to the hallway, she's leaning against the wall, facing away from me. I put my hand on her back gently.

"What's wrong?" I ask.

Her breath is coming in short bursts, almost like she's going to hyperventilate or something. "I did something really bad to someone," she says.

"Who?"

"Derrick." She wipes at her eyes with the back of her hand. Then she sort of half slides/half collapses onto the floor. So she *is* cheating on him. With whoever that was at the door. What is up with everyone cheating lately? It must be because it's the end of our senior year. Everyone's getting restless in their relationships.

Still. I can't be mad at her. I don't know anything about her situation with Derrick, what their relationship is like. And besides, I want a chance to prove myself, to show Lyla I care about her, that I can be there for her when she needs me, that she shouldn't have just cut me out of her life like she did.

"Stay here," I tell her.

Then I go to the vending machine and buy two cans of Sprite and a king-size package of peanut butter cups. I'm kind of nervous that maybe she won't be there when I get back, but she's exactly where I left her, sitting on the floor, her back against the wall and her legs sticking out at a weird angle that definitely can't be comfortable.

"Thanks," she says, taking the soda from me and popping the top.

"You're welcome." I don't say anything else, hoping she's going to volunteer some information about what's going on with her. But she doesn't, so after a second I say, "So what did you do?"

But she shakes her head. "I don't want to talk about it."

My heart sinks a tiny bit, because I had this mental picture of us sitting out here in the hall while she confided in me and we mended our friendship. But if she doesn't want to talk about it, I have to respect that. "Okay." I offer her a peanut butter cup, and she takes it. Besides, whatever bad thing she's done isn't even that important—it's whether it can be fixed that matters. "Well, do you think it can be fixed?" I ask.

"I don't know," she says.

I nod and nibble at my peanut butter cup.

And then, suddenly, Lyla says something that totally throws me for a loop. "Did you tell Liam you're in love with him?"

"You remembered," I say, surprised. "About my email. What I wanted to do."

"Of course I remembered," she says.

I smile, but Lyla rolls her eyes.

"Don't get so excited," she says. "It's not like it's something I could forget. You've been in love with Liam since forever."

She's right. I don't know why I thought that maybe her remembering meant something. I talked about Liam so much when Lyla and Quinn and I were still friends that she couldn't have forgotten even if she wanted to.

"No," I admit. "I haven't told him yet. But I'm going to." I don't know why I'm saying that, when I just pretty much decided I *wasn't* going to. I think it's because I want Lyla to feel like we have something in common, like we're both doing hard things together. She'll tell Derrick the truth about whatever it was she was doing with whoever it was she was doing it with, and I'll tell Liam the truth about how I feel.

It will be like Lyla and I are in it together, which is kind of how those emails were supposed to be in the first place— the three of us were supposed to confront our fears as a unit.

"And honestly, Lyla," I go on, "you should tell Derrick the truth. You're not going to be able to work out whatever it is unless you tell him."

I wait for her to say something, but she doesn't.

She just stays quiet.

She has a contemplative look on her face, though, and at least she's not yelling at me and telling me to stay the hell out of her business, so I guess it's some sort of progress. But still. I *miss* her. I miss her *so much*. I wish I was going to break-fast with her and not Izzy, that we were going to be sitting in a cozy booth together, ordering pancakes and listening to island music before spending the day on the beach, away from our problems.

I think about pushing her a little, trying to get her to confide in me, but I don't want to ruin whatever inroads I might have made. So I gather up the empty candy wrappers and then stand up. "I'm going to go grab breakfast." I squeeze her shoulder. "Good luck."

God knows we're both going to need it.

Twenty minutes later, I'm at the restaurant where I'm supposed to meet Izzy. It's called the Splattered Egg, and it's cute, albeit a total tourist trap. Palm trees flank both sides of the sidewalk, and there's a huge outdoor eating area with people sitting at brightly colored wicker tables.

Izzy's already there, settled into a table in the corner, one of the only ones that doesn't have an umbrella. She's wearing big black sunglasses, a cream-colored tank top, and khaki shorts. A gauzy black beach wrap is slung around her shoulders. Her hair cascades down her shoulders in waves, and the sun glints off her curls. She looks like a movie star trying to avoid the paparazzi.

I'm wearing a navy-blue tank top and denim shorts, white flip-flops that are a little dirty from the beach yesterday, and my hair is in a messy ponytail. My bag is a black-and-gray-striped tote from Walmart.

Izzy smiles when she sees me, and puts a napkin in the book she's reading to hold her place.

"Hi," I say, sliding into the seat across from her. "You look pretty."

"Thanks."

"How'd you get a table so quick?" I ask. The sidewalk is filled with people waiting for a seat.

Izzy waves her hand. "I've been here for a while," she says, gesturing to the orange juice and half-empty cup of coffee that are sitting in front of her. "Just reading."

"Oh." I want to tell her it might not have been the best idea to take up a table when there are so many people waiting, but I don't. It wouldn't be nice, and besides, it's too late now.

Then my eyes fall on her book. It's our book club book. Me and Liam's. *Someday, Someday, Maybe.*

"Oh," I say, surprised. "You're reading that?"

"Yeah." She sighs. "I decided that if Liam and I are going to work through our problems, I should probably start being more into the kind of stuff he's into. So I guess I'm joining your book club."

I'm annoyed. I know it's petty—why shouldn't Izzy be allowed to join if she wants?—but the book club belongs to me and Liam. We started it way before Izzy even moved to our school district, way before she showed up and started dating Liam. It's our thing, the place we go to connect, to debate, to share opinions. Not that we need an excuse to do those things, of course, but it's just . . . Izzy's going to upset the whole dynamic. Liam and I have years of private jokes and rituals built up around this stuff. Izzy can't come in and expect to just get it.

And what, is she going to be allowed to start picking books? The whole point of book club is for me to force Liam to read girly books, and for Liam to force me to read something awful. Like when he made me read *Sarah's Key*, this book about the Holocaust that I'm pretty sure was based on a true story. I kept waiting for the book to turn around and have a happy ending, but it didn't. It was just one big depressing mess.

Liam said I needed to open my mind to things that have gone on in the world, and that just because some of those things might be depressing didn't mean I should shy away from them. But now that Izzy's joining our club, is he going to tease her like that, too? Or is she going to agree with him?

I have a vision of the two of them making me read some book on World War II or something and then ganging up on me and making me feel like I don't care about anything that's important, that I'm dumb for wanting to read books with happy endings. I read to escape my problems, not start thinking about someone else's, thank you very much. But now the whole meeting is going to be the two of them bullying me, and then maybe at the end Izzy will climb into

Liam's lap and they'll make out in front of me. Wow. Book club's really going to suck from now on.

"Did Liam invite you to join book club?" I ask carefully.

"No," she says. "But he's—" She lowers her voice and looks around. "Moody," she whispers.

"Oh." I look around, too. "Why are you whispering?"

"Because it's private," she says.

"Okay. So what happened?"

"We had a horrible night!" she says. "He came to the star walk, and we ended up getting into a fight."

"About what?" I ask. I wonder if I should tell her Liam and I got into a fight, too. On one hand, it's not really any of her business, and besides, I don't really feel like talking about it. On the other hand, why wouldn't I bring it up? And what if Liam already told her? Won't she think it's weird if I don't mention it?

"Well, first, he showed up all moody," she says. "I'm not sure, but I think something happened at Juliana's party that made him upset."

So he *didn't* tell her we got into a fight. I pick up my menu and study it intently, stalling for time while I debate in my head—tell Izzy that Liam and I got into an argument, and that it might have had something to do with his bad mood? Or don't say anything and hope that she doesn't find out later and wonder why I never mentioned it?

"Oh," I manage. I feel like I'm saying "oh" a lot. Does Izzy realize I've been saying "oh" a lot? Suddenly I'm very aware of the sun beating down on me from overhead. Why didn't Izzy pick a table with an umbrella? I look around to see if there's another table we can ask to switch to, but they're all full. I pick up my water and take a small sip.

"Are you okay?" Izzy asks. "You're being weird."

"No, I'm not," I say.

"You kind of are. You're—" She reaches across the table and grabs my arm. "Oh God!" she says, the color draining from her face. "Liam's here. Just act natural."

"Liam's here?" I ask. That's impossible. What are the chances Liam would show up at the exact same restaurant as us at the exact same time? It's a big island. Plus, Liam hates going out to breakfast. He thinks any time before noon is too early to get out of bed.

I start to turn around.

"Don't turn around!" Izzy shrieks.

"But are you sure it's him? What is he doing here?"

"I invited him."

"You *what?*"

"I invited him to breakfast." Izzy takes off her sunglasses and starts polishing them with her napkin. Then she puts them back on, sliding them up onto her head. They pull her hair back from her face, making her look younger than she is.

"*Why?*"

"Because I need to make up with him. I need things to go back to the way they were."

"Then why did you invite *me*?"

"So you could defuse the tension."

"I can't . . . I mean, I'm not really up for defusing anything, tension or otherwise."

"But—oh, shh! Here he comes!"

A second later, Liam slides into the seat next to me. I don't look at him, but my heart speeds up and my stomach flips. He's so close I can smell the spiciness of his cologne, the freshness of his soap, the fruitiness of his sunscreen.

"Hey," he says. I can't tell if he's talking to Izzy or me or both of us. He doesn't sound upset, which I guess is good.

"Hi," I say. I look up from my menu and our eyes meet. I catch my breath and my pulse starts racing. Something passes between us, a frisson of electricity, something alive and exciting. I can tell from the look on his face that he hasn't told Izzy about our fight. We have a secret. A secret from Izzy. We've never had that before. It's thrilling and scary and exciting and terrifying.

"So," I say, struggling to keep my voice even. "Uh, what's good to eat here?"

"I'm getting pancakes," Izzy announces boldly, like she's waiting for someone to tell her she can't.

"French toast," Liam says without even looking at the menu. He gets French toast anytime we're at a twenty-four-hour diner, when we go out for a late breakfast, or on rare occasions like this, where we've somehow managed to drag him out of bed before the afternoon.

"Are you sure?" I tease, figuring I might as well embrace my role as tension-defuser. "You haven't had that in a while."

"True," he says, pretending to think about it. "I'm going to switch it up today and get some bacon with my French toast."

It's a joke. Liam always gets bacon with his French toast. I smile, glad he's not going to hold a grudge about our fight. I mean, obviously we're going to have to talk about it at some point—we can't just pretend it didn't happen. But at least it's not going to be weird until we're able to work it out. I let out a sigh of relief.

But Izzy's not having it.

"You always get bacon," she says, and she sounds irritated.

"He likes what he likes," I say simply. I take another sip of my water, then try to move on before Izzy can get going. "I'd like some orange juice, though. Izzy, which one is our waitress?"

"Yeah, he likes what he likes until he doesn't like it anymore," Izzy says sourly.

"What's that supposed to mean?" Liam asks, frowning.

"Nothing. Just that you pretend to be loyal until you're not."

Oh. My. God. What is she *doing?* She's talking like a crazy person. If she wanted to confront Liam about what she found in his phone, this is definitely not the way to do it. And if she *has* decided to do it this way, she definitely shouldn't be doing it in front of me.

"I have no idea what you're talking about," Liam says. He sounds like he really doesn't, either. He glances at me, like he's looking for some kind of clue as to what Izzy's talking about. But there's no way I'm getting involved in their drama.

I shrug and give what I hope is a confused-looking smile. "Where is that waitress?" I ask. "All these tourist places think they can get away with having bad service because they don't need to keep any regular customers." I cluck my tongue, which I've never done before. Like, ever. I sound like someone's grandmother. It really shows how much stress I'm under. A young girl who probably doesn't even work at the restaurant wanders by, and I flag her down. "Excuse me," I say frantically, "but can we get some juice for our table?"

She scrunches up her face and just walks away, without even explaining that she doesn't work there.

"I don't think she works here," Izzy says kindly, apparently saving her wrath for Liam and Liam alone.

Our waitress comes over then, the real one, and she gives us a smile. "Hello!" she says brightly. "Would you like to start with a Bloody Mary or a mimosa?" Um, does she not realize that we're not twenty-one? Some of us aren't even eighteen. And besides, the last thing this situation needs is alcohol. Everyone here is already acting crazy enough.

Izzy frowns, like she's actually considering it.

"No, that's okay," I say quickly. "We're all just going to have orange juice."

"Great!" the waitress says. "I'll be right back with those." I'm not sure if it's my imagination but I think she gives Liam an extra-special smile before she walks away. Doesn't she realize Liam has enough problems? He's already in trouble trying to juggle Izzy and Annabelle, how is he going to add a random waitress into the mix?

"I wanted a mimosa," Izzy mumbles once the waitress is gone.

"You're not twenty-one," I point out, and take another sip of my water.

"Yeah, but she wasn't going to ID us. She suggested it. Nobody IDs at brunch."

It's not true—I've had brunch out plenty of times and seen people getting ID'd. At least, I think I have.

"And besides," Izzy goes on, "I didn't want orange juice at all."

"You just said you wanted a mimosa," I say.

"So?"

"So a mimosa has orange juice."

"Yes, but if I couldn't have alcohol in my orange juice, I

wanted something else." She's tapping her nails against her menu, all agitated.

"Okay," I say, annoyed that she's acting this way but really wanting to keep the peace. "We'll just call the waitress back over here and change our order."

"No," Izzy says. "It's too late." She tilts her head down and starts scanning the menu. She hugs her arms close to her, bending over a little bit until her hair falls over her face. I glance at Liam, wondering what he's thinking about this whole thing, but he's on his phone, texting. To Annabelle? I pretend to be looking around for the waitress and try to get a glimpse of his screen. But I can't see anything.

"I'm going to get an omelet," Izzy says.

"Really?" I ask. "I thought you were a vegetarian."

"I am," Izzy says. "Vegetarians can eat eggs, Aven. Some even eat chicken or fish."

I frown. "I think that's called a flexitarian." I turn to Liam, who's still typing away on his phone. "Liam and I read a book about it." He doesn't say anything, so I keep babbling on. "Well, it wasn't *just* about being pescatarian, it was this book about the food industry and how, you know, things are being put into our food supply that are gross. And, like, GMOs." Izzy stares at me blankly, and Liam's not even looking at me. "And how we're not supposed to eat processed foods." By the end of the sentence my voice has a bit of an edge to it, and I'm sounding kind of hysterical.

Which is unfortunate, because I'm supposed to be the calm one here, the one who's smoothing everything over. But you'd think the two of them could help me at least a little. Izzy's being annoying and combative, and Liam's just sitting there texting on his phone and ignoring us.

"You know," I say to him, "you're being kind of rude."

He still doesn't respond, so I reach over and poke him in the upper arm. He's holding his phone in such a way that his bicep is flexed, and even though I'm mad at him, I can't help noticing how ripped he is. I remember yesterday, the two of us on the beach, Liam with his shirt off, me up on his shoulders, reaching down and holding on to his chin, how strong he felt under me, how his stubble felt under my fingers. Even though I'm frustrated with him right now, I'm somehow still completely and totally attracted to him. Which makes me even more frustrated.

I poke him again, a little harder this time.

He looks up, surprised. "Did you just poke me?"

"Yes. I just poked you. Because you're being incredibly rude."

"How am I being rude?" It's one of those questions boys ask when they know exactly what they're doing but just feel like being difficult.

"You're ignoring us for your phone," I say. "If you come to brunch with people, you should put your phone away and enjoy their company."

"Sorry," he says. He doesn't sound sorry. But he puts his phone away.

Izzy crosses her arms over her chest and sits back in her chair. "God forbid you have to put your phone down for a minute. You wouldn't want to miss any important *business* you have on it." She looks at me with an expectant look, like she's hoping I'm going to back her up. Why would she think I was going to back her up? She's the one who looked in his phone. And again, if she's going to start confronting Liam about what she's found out, she really shouldn't be doing it in public. And definitely not in front of me. I have no place in this conversation.

"What's that supposed to mean?" Liam asks, frowning. "I hardly ever use my phone when we're out."

It's true. Liam's usually very respectful when it comes to being distracted by his phone. But maybe Annabelle's changed all that. Maybe he can't stand to be away from her for even one second, so he's constantly texting her. Maybe they're sexting. Not now, of course. I don't think Liam would be dumb enough to sext out at breakfast with his girlfriend sitting right next to him. Talk about reckless.

"Well, apparently things have changed. Right, Aven?" Izzy asks ominously. She's giving me that same expectant look, and a feeling of dread washes over me.

I realize now why she invited me to brunch, why she didn't tell me Liam was coming. She wanted to ambush us. Well, him. She's going to bring up the whole Annabelle thing, and she wants me for reinforcement. What she didn't count on, though, is that Liam and I are fighting ourselves— so Liam isn't going to be too excited to hear my opinion on anything, especially his secret text buddy.

And how exactly does Izzy plan on bringing Annabelle up, anyway? Is she going to admit she looked in Liam's phone? And if so, is she really expecting me to pretend I'm okay with that? Because I'm not. And I've *told* Izzy that a bunch of times. In fact, all I've been saying this whole time is that she should ask Liam about her concerns, and that it was totally wrong for her to look in his phone.

Obviously she wasn't listening.

She might be coming a little unhinged, honestly.

I take another sip of my water.

"You know what," I say, trying to make my voice sound weak. "I'm not feeling so good." I push my chair back from the table. "I think I better go back to the hotel."

"What's wrong?" Liam asks, concerned. "Are you okay?"

"Oh, yeah, I'm fine," I say. "I just—"

"Okay!" the waitress crows, setting three glasses of juice down on the table. "Orange juice for everyone!" She pulls her pad out of her apron. "Are you guys ready to order?"

"Yes," Izzy says. "I'm going to have an omelet with mushrooms and cheese. Wheat toast, no butter, slightly well done."

"The omelet or the toast?"

"The toast."

The waitress turns to Liam. "And for you?"

"French toast, side of bacon, side of fruit salad."

She writes it down. "And you?" she asks me.

"Oh, um—"

"She's not feeling well," Izzy interrupts. "So she's just going to have some oatmeal. And can we get her a hot tea, too?"

Great. Now my fake illness has cost me a delicious breakfast.

When the waitress leaves, Liam turns back to me. "Are you okay? Do you need to go back to the hotel? Come on, I'll walk you."

"Relax," Izzy says. "She's not sick. She just doesn't want to be here when I confront you." She sighs. "Look, I want to talk about this like adults." She turns and looks at me. "And, Aven, I want you here to help meditate things."

"Meditate? I think you mean mediate."

"Yeah, that's what I said." Izzy folds her hands in front of her. "Mediate."

"What are you talking about?" Liam asks. "Why does she need to mediate anything?"

"Because this might turn into a fight," Izzy says calmly.

"You guys," I say quickly. "This is really not my business."

"What's going to turn into a fight?" Liam asks.

"When I ask you about Annabelle."

Oh my God. Oh my God! She's doing it! She's actually doing it! And it's not even in the heat of the moment or anything, she just completely blurted it out like it was nothing.

"Annabelle?" Liam frowns.

"Yes, Annabelle." Izzy repeats it with a mean sort of look on her face and then sits back in her chair. "We know all about her."

"Uh, well, I don't," I say quickly. "I mean, I just know what Izzy's told me."

"What Izzy's told you?" Liam repeats.

"Stop repeating everything we're saying," Izzy commands.

I'm slightly panicked by the fact that she keeps referring to us as a "we." "We" weren't the one who looked in Liam's phone while he was walking down the beach. "We" weren't the one who was so nervous he was cheating on her that she freaked out and started questioning him.

"I think I should go," I say.

"No, I think you should stay," Liam says, giving me a look like he knows exactly what I'm trying to do. "I really want to hear what you two have to say, and how you know about Annabelle."

"I don't really know about her," I say. "I told you, I just know, ah, what Izzy told me."

"And Izzy?" Liam asks, turning to her. "What do you know about Annabelle?"

"I know that you're having a clandestine affair with her!" Izzy says. She goes to grab for Liam's phone, like she wants to pull up the proof, but he moves it out of her reach. He does it very calmly, like he could actually care less about her seeing what's in it, that it's more just a matter of principle. He doesn't seem worried that he might have been caught doing something wrong. In fact, Izzy's the one who seems frantic. Like, she's trying to appear calm, but you can tell she's totally spiraling.

"A clandestine affair?" Liam repeats. "You cannot be serious."

"Of course I'm serious!" Izzy says. "And I asked you to please stop repeating everything I said."

"You didn't ask me, actually," Liam says. "You ordered me."

"Listen," I say, "guys, I'm sure this is just a misunderstanding. There's probably some really good explanation for the whole Annabelle thing." I turn to Liam. "Right, Liam?"

"Hold on a second," Liam says, shaking his head. "You never answered my original question. *How* do you two know about Annabelle?"

"I heard it from Izzy," I say quickly.

"How I found out isn't important," Izzy says vaguely.

But of course it is important. It's important because if

Izzy has to tell Liam how she found out, then he's going to have a reason to be mad at her. He'll question her and she'll try to deflect and then—

"But if you must know, I went through your phone," Izzy declares.

"Oh, Izzy," I breathe, and put my head in my hands. Not that I think admitting it is necessarily a bad thing. It's just that she's going about this whole thing the completely wrong way. If she was going to admit she'd gone through his phone, she should have led with how she felt like something was off with their relationship. Then she could have told Liam she went through his phone, and that she was really sorry but that she was so upset she didn't know what else to do. You can't just blurt out the fact that you went through someone's phone like that and expect them to be okay with it.

"You went through my phone?" Liam asks. He takes in a deep breath through his nose, and his jaw sets into a firm line. "Wow, Izzy, that was a gross invasion of my privacy."

"Looking through someone's phone is nowhere near as bad as cheating," Izzy says, like she's the moral police or something. "So if you want to start pointing fingers at people, maybe you should start pointing them at yourself."

"Izzy—" I start, but she's not done.

"And obviously I was right to look in your phone, because I found something incriminating!" She goes to reach for his phone again, and Liam pulls it out of the way.

"Izzy," I say, starting to get worried about how crazy she's acting, "why don't you and Liam go back to the hotel and have a nice, normal conversation about this? I bet if you talk to each other like adults, this can all be worked out."

"Cheating is a deal breaker!" Izzy says.

"Yeah, well, so is looking through my phone," Liam says.

"Then I guess there's nothing else to say," Izzy says.

"I guess not."

"I guess we're breaking up," Izzy says.

My pulse starts to pound, and goose bumps break out on my arms. Breaking up? Like, for *real* breaking up? I don't know how I'm supposed to feel about that. On one hand, I'm excited. On the other hand, I don't want Izzy to be sad. I don't want *Liam* to be sad. Although in my darkest moments, when I've let myself really go there, when it's late at night and I'm alone in my bed and allowing myself to think about no one but myself, I don't care if Liam and Izzy are sad. I *want* them to break up. I do. I can't help it.

"I guess we are," Liam says quietly.

There's a silence, where I think maybe both of them are waiting for the other one to take it back, or at least say they should talk about it. But neither one of them does.

"Maybe you guys should talk about this," I offer after a moment. It may seem counterintuitive to the fact that I want them to break up. But when you think about it, it makes perfect sense. Why would I want to get my hopes up over a fake breakup? A fake breakup would be worse than no breakup at all.

"There's nothing to talk about," Izzy says. She slides her sunglasses down over her eyes. "I'm leaving."

"No, don't go," I say halfheartedly, hoping she won't listen. How awesome would it be for Izzy to leave and me to be left here with Liam, just the two of us? He wouldn't have a girlfriend anymore.

Before graduation, I will . . . tell the truth.

There wouldn't be a reason not to. I could tell him right here, right now. I could tell him how I feel, that I can't stop thinking about him, that ever since the moment I met him I've had a crush on him, and then it turned deeper and now I might be in love with him. I could point out all the things we have in common, all the time we've spent together, all the reasons we would be perfect together.

"She's right," Liam says. "You don't have to leave, Izzy. Because I am." He pushes his chair away from the table and stands up a little too quickly. His orange juice jostles on the table and sloshes over the side.

And then he's gone.

I turn to Izzy.

"Wow," I say, letting out the breath I didn't realize I was holding. "That was intense."

"What an asshole," Izzy says. "Can you believe he admitted to cheating on me and then had the nerve to get mad at me for going through his phone?"

I frown. "He didn't really admit he was cheating," I say, realizing it's true. "All he said was, 'How do you know about Annabelle?'"

"Which is admitting it," Izzy says. "If he wasn't cheating on me, he would have been like, 'I'm not cheating on you.'"

Or maybe he didn't want to have to justify himself to you after you looked in his phone, I want to say, but don't. Izzy is worked up enough already. And besides, maybe she has a point. Why didn't Liam just tell her who Annabelle is? He didn't look guilty, though, like he'd been caught. He looked more pissed off than anything.

"I have a headache," Izzy says suddenly, putting her hand to her head. She sniffs at her orange juice. "I hope this wasn't made in a facility that manufactures peanuts."

"I'm sure it wasn't." Why would they be making orange juice in a place that manufactures peanuts?

"It probably was," she says. "Even though the menu claimed it was fresh-squeezed." She reaches into her bag, pulls out a prescription bottle, and shakes two pills into her hand. "You'd be surprised at how often places misrepresent what they're serving."

"Totally," I say, even though I'm not sure I agree with her.

"I'm going to have a migraine now," she says. "Great. Just great."

She's probably going to have a migraine not because of

the peanuts but because of the fact that she and Liam just had a very public fight and then apparently broke up. Stress can cause migraines, can't it? And what are the chances some fresh-squeezed orange juice ended up with peanuts in it? It really doesn't make any sense.

"I'm sorry," I say. "Is there anything I can do?"

"Yes." She reaches across the table and grabs my forearm like it's a life raft. "You can stay here and pay the bill. I need to get back to my room."

She stands up and shoulders her bag.

"Are you sure you should be going by yourself?" I ask, looking around for the waitress. "Let me go with you."

"No, no, I'll be fine. Sometimes if I lie down before it gets going, it helps ward it off."

"Okay," I say doubtfully. I'm not sure I should let her go alone, but a second later, she's gone.

She probably went to find Liam, anyway. He's probably going to be waiting for her outside her room, and they're probably going to end up talking it out. They'll be back together before dinner.

They might not be, a tempting little voice in my head whispers. Coming back from someone possibly cheating and the other person breaking their trust is going to be really hard. Even if they try to work through it, they could still split up. And if Liam really *is* cheating on Izzy, then they're probably done.

On the other hand, if Liam and Izzy *do* break up, then this Annabelle person might be Liam's new girlfriend. And who knows what she's like. At least with Izzy, I knew what I was getting—she could be annoying sometimes, yes, but she was my friend, too, and she never saw me as a threat. She didn't care if I hung out with Liam until all hours of the night, if we had a book club and our own private jokes.

She looked at me the same way she'd look at one of Liam's guy friends. Sometimes I think she was even secretly relieved Liam and I were so close, because it made her feel less guilty when she wanted to hang out with her dance team or do something Liam wasn't interested in.

But Annabelle is a total question mark. She could be one of those completely jealous girls who doesn't want their boyfriend to do anything except be with her. She might not like the fact that Liam has me as a friend. She might see me as a threat, she might force him to make a decision—her or me.

And even though I know Liam would never intentionally just throw our friendship away, what if it happens unintentionally? What if now that they're not a secret affair, Liam and Annabelle can start spending all their time in public, out and about as a couple? What if slowly Liam and I just start drifting apart until finally we're not even speaking? First our book club meetings will get further and further apart, then they'll stop altogether. He'll stop sending me his music. I'll stop writing my book, the one that's about us. Or I'll have to give it a horrible ending, one where the two people don't end up together.

Because it won't feel right to write the ending I want unless it actually happens. Of course I'll have to make sure it seems like the girl is okay even without the guy, that she's realized she can find someone better or work on her dreams or something. But none of the readers will believe it, because everyone will know her heart is still broken and that she's never going to be the same.

Wow. My book is really going to suck. It's definitely not going to sell with an ending like that. Readers want a happily ever after. And the reason they want a happily ever after is because they want an escape. They want something to happen in a book that's never going to happen to them in real life. At the same time, they want to feel like maybe it *could*, like maybe they're going to be the exception to the rule.

Which is what I wanted.

Which is why I was writing that particular kind of book!

"Okay, here we go," the waitress says, returning to the table with our food. "French toast, omelet, and oatmeal." She sets everything down with a flourish and gives me a smile. "Can I get you anything else?"

Sigh.

* * *

I pay the bill and then head back to the hotel.

I'm slightly annoyed that I had to pay for everyone's food, even though it was just breakfast. They're the ones who dragged me to the restaurant—well, Izzy did at least—under false pretenses, then made it really uncomfortable for me while they had a fight and broke up, so to stick me with the bill on top of it . . . Ugh.

Not to mention that now I have nothing to do for the rest of the day. I mean, I guess I could call Reva from the Student Action Committee, but come on. I really do not want to be spending my vacation with her. She's nice enough, but she's not Liam and Izzy.

Liam and Izzy.

Izzy and Liam.

I'm so sick of hearing their names together. I picture the two of them back at her room. Are they making up? Is he taking care of her since she has a migraine? Is he promising never to see Annabelle again? Or is Liam relieved Izzy found out, is he alone talking to Annabelle right now, telling her the good news, that he finally got rid of his girlfriend?

I take the elevator up to the second floor, hoping against hope that Quinn and Lyla aren't in our room. I'm emotionally exhausted, and the last thing I want is a run-in with those two. I'm hunched over and looking at the floor while I walk, which is why I don't see him at first.

Liam.

He's waiting outside my door, sitting on the floor, his head back against the wall, his hands resting on his knees. Longing and want flow through my body, the way they do sometimes when I least expect it, when nothing's happening except that he's near me, or I catch him looking at me a certain way, or my hand brushes against his arm.

"Hey," he says when he sees me.

"Hey," I breathe.

"Can we talk?" He stands up and moves toward me.

"Sure," I say. "Um, do you want to come into my room?"

He shakes his head. "I'm too keyed up to stay inside. You wanna go for a walk?"

I nod. "Beach?"

He nods back and starts walking down the hall.

Before graduation, I will . . . tell the truth.

"You coming?" Liam asks.

"Yeah." I take a deep breath and follow him.

EIGHT

THE BEACH IS PRETTY BUSY, BUT EVERYONE is congregating around the center of the coast, up where the pavilion and the food stand are located. So Liam and I walk silently until we find a spot all the way down the shore. There's a wall that curves up from the ground to protect the oceanfront houses from trespassers, and right behind it are a bunch of palm trees casting a bit of shade onto the beach. So I pick a patch of shade for myself and sit down near the wall, up where the sand is rocky and not as smooth.

"Do you mind if we sit farther down?" Liam asks, gesturing toward the shore. "I kind of want to be closer to the water."

"Sure." I move into the sun and we both sit down right in the sand, no blanket or umbrella or anything. I slip my sandals off and let the tide slide over my toes. The water is cold, but the air is hot, so they kind of cancel each other out. I remember what Liam said about vitamin D, so I raise my face to the sun and hope I'm soaking some up.

I wait for Liam to say something, and when he doesn't, I glance over at him. He's staring out at the water, his face contemplative, his chin resting on his hand, his thumb moving back and forth over his bottom lip, like he's trying to work something out in his head.

I pick up a stick and doodle a little bit in the sand, just nonsense things, my name, a heart, one of those five point stars you can make without picking up your pen. I draw a tic-tac-toe board and play a game with myself until Liam notices what I'm doing.

"Are you playing tic-tac-toe with yourself?" he asks.

"Yes."

"Why?"

"Why not? This way I always win."

He grins and takes the stick out of my hand. He draws a new board on the sand in between us and then hands the stick back to me.

"Your move," he says, and his fingers brush against mine. A breeze rustles through the palm trees overhead, and maybe I've been reading too many romance novels or maybe I've just finally gone insane, but it feels like something's different, like there's been a subtle shift between us. I can't explain it, but it's there.

"No way," I say, shaking my head. "You get the first move."

"You sure?" he asks.

"I'm sure," I say, raising my chin. "I'm not scared."

He draws an *O* in the middle square.

I shake my head. "Taking the easy way out, eh, Marsh?"

I draw an *X* in the upper middle square and then hand him back the stick. Every time we pass it back and forth, our hands are going to touch. With nine squares on the board, that could be a lot of touching.

"So I wanted to explain to you," he says, drawing an *O* in the lower left square, "about Annabelle."

"Okay," I say. "But honestly, Liam, you don't have to explain anything to me." It's true—as much as I want to know about this whole Annabelle thing, it really isn't any of my business. If Liam has a secret girlfriend, it would suck and break my heart—but he doesn't have an obligation to tell me about it unless he wants to.

"No, I want to."

"Okay." I draw my *X* and hand him back the stick. But he doesn't draw another *O*. Instead he takes the stick and just kind of moves it back and forth across the sand in a lazy swirly pattern.

"I'm not cheating on Izzy," he says. "Annabelle isn't a girl."

"Annabelle's a boy?" I ask, confused.

He laughs. "No, Annabelle's a girl. Well, a woman, actually. I just meant she's not a girl that I'm, like, romantically involved with or anything."

"Oh. She's a friend?"

"No. She's my therapist." He turns and looks at me, waiting for my reaction. Which, honestly, is one of relief. Annabelle's not a girlfriend! She's isn't even a friend! She's his therapist! Wow. Talk about much ado about nothing.

Wait. Since when does Liam see a therapist? And why didn't he just tell Izzy about it?

"I didn't know you were seeing a therapist," I say.

"That's because I didn't tell you," he says.

"Why not?"

He shrugs and looks back out across the water. He's having trouble meeting my gaze while we're talking about this, and I realize it's because it's hard for him. "Embarrassed, I guess."

"Why? Lots of people see therapists."

"I don't know. It just seems like kind of a weird thing to do. I'm a grown man, I shouldn't be seeing a therapist."

I grin. "It's not weird. And don't worry, you're not a grown man."

He laughs and turns back to the game, putting an *O* in one of the top squares. His *O* isn't closed at the top, and something about it seems almost metaphorical.

"So, um, why are you seeing a therapist?"

"Just, you know, stuff with my dad."

I take the stick and draw another *X*. "Is he going with you?"

"What do you think?"

I nod. There's no way Liam's dad is going with him to therapy. Liam doesn't talk about his dad much—his parents divorced when he was thirteen, and I think Liam feels abandoned by him, even though from what he's told me, he was better off with his dad out of the house. His dad never hit him—at least, not that Liam told me—but he was extremely verbally abusive to both him and his mom.

Liam still has a relationship with his dad, though—he sees him every other weekend. His dad doesn't care about things like Liam's music, or the fact that Liam was all-state in lacrosse without even really trying. Mr. Marsh thinks all that stuff is a waste of time. He's always trying to take Liam hunting or sailing, things Liam has no interest in.

"Do you want to talk about it?" I ask carefully.

Liam takes the stick and draws an *O* in the middle left square on our board, winning the game. He draws a line down over the *O*s, signifying his win, then scratches out another empty board and hands me the stick.

"I'm just struggling a little," he says. "It's nothing horrible or anything. It's just all the normal conflicted feelings. Like how can I still want to please him when he's been nothing but an asshole to me? And how come I feel guilty if I don't want to see him, like it's my fault and I'm not being a good son?"

"Probably because he lays a guilt trip on you." The one time I ever met Liam's dad, he showed up at one of Liam's lacrosse games at the beginning of the second half and expected Liam to leave with him. When Liam said no, that he had plans with the rest of the team to go to lunch afterward, his dad called him an ungrateful little punk and stomped off the field. Everyone heard it, and it was really embarrassing for Liam.

"Yeah. And I know that. So then why do I care?"

"Because he's your dad."

"Still."

"Yeah." I think about it while I draw a soft, smooth *X* into the middle square. "I guess that's what Annabelle is going to help you figure out."

"Yup." He sighs. "Anyway. So that's who Annabelle is."

"Well, I'm glad you told me."

"Really?" he asks. "You're not mad that I've been keeping it a secret?"

I shake my head. "Sometimes it's okay to keep things to yourself until you figure out how you feel about them."

"Thanks." He draws another *O* on the board, the same kind that's not closed on top, but he doesn't seem to be paying attention to the game anymore. So when he hands the stick back to me, I set it down on the sand. The tide is moving farther out, and the waves aren't hitting my toes now, so I scooch a little farther down the sand to get my feet back into the water.

Liam abandons our game and comes to sit next to me. There's a boat out in the distance, with someone parasailing off the back, and we sit there watching for a while as the red-and-white-striped parachute flutters through the air and the sunlight glints off the ocean, making the water look almost silver.

"You okay?" I ask after a second. "You're being quiet."

"Yeah, I'm fine." But he doesn't sound fine. He's back in that same position again, his hand on his chin, his thumb moving over his lower lip, back and forth, back and forth.

"Are you sure? Are you upset because Izzy went through your phone?"

"No. I mean, yeah, I'm upset about that. It wasn't right for her to do it, but she . . . I don't want to make excuses for her, but part of me can't really blame her. I haven't been myself around her lately, and so it's only natural she would go looking for reasons."

"Was it because of Annabelle?" I ask. "That you were being weird around Izzy?" Although now that I'm thinking about it, that really wouldn't make any sense. Why would the fact that Liam was seeing a therapist make him act weird around Izzy? Unless for some reason he was bringing up his relationship with Izzy in therapy, and something Annabelle said made him feel strange about him and Izzy. But Liam said he was in therapy because of his dad. So why would he be talking to Annabelle about Izzy?

"No, it's not because of Annabelle." He shakes his head, and then very slowly, he turns toward me. His eyes lock onto mine, and there's something in them I've never seen before. Confusion. Not that I've never seen Liam look confused before—when he's working on a new song, when I'm trying to explain to him why I like a certain book, that way, when we get a new set of problems in precalc—but this confusion is different. It's . . . I don't know. *Deeper* is the only way I can describe it.

A little thrill skitters up my spine.

"Then why?" I ask.

"Don't you think it's weird that I'm here talking to you?"

I frown. "Is this one of those existential questions?" Every so often Liam will bust out with some crazy life riddle, like how it's impossible for God to exist, because if God's omnipotent, then he should be able to create something more powerful than himself, which actually wouldn't make him omnipotent after all. He usually gets me all caught up in debating him, and we can sometimes end up talking about the same thing for hours.

"No." He shakes his head, and his gaze is still locked onto mine. "I mean don't you think it's weird that I'm here talking to you and not Izzy?"

I shrug. "Not really. I mean, you and Izzy are in a fight." *And you broke up.* Except I don't say that last part out loud, because I don't want to hear him say they haven't. Especially now that I know Annabelle's not some vixen-y mistress.

"Right. So wouldn't it have made more sense for me to go to Izzy's room and wait for *her*? So we could talk, so I could explain things to her?"

"Maybe you just needed some time to think about what you wanted to tell her," I say, my pulse pounding. But my voice sounds small, like I'm talking from far away.

"I didn't. When I left that table, I wanted to get back to the hotel so I could see *you*, so I could explain things to *you*. I didn't want you to think I was a cheater or a liar."

"We're best friends. It makes sense." My voice still has that faraway quality to it, and now on top of that, I can hear the sound of my own heart beating, the blood rushing through my body. I feel like something is happening, something out of my control. It's like someone's been slowly moving tiny little rocks away from a huge boulder and now finally, the boulder is starting to tumble down the mountain and there's no way to stop it.

"It makes sense that I would get into a huge fight with my girlfriend, and all I would be able to think about is how I didn't want you to think I was a liar?" Liam asks softly.

Before graduation, I will . . . tell the truth.

He's looking right at me.

He's looking right at me, and the waves are coming in and we're in this beautiful place, on a beach for God's sakes, and it's just me and him and I remember how it felt just a minute ago when we were playing tic-tac-toe, passing that stick back and forth, his hand against mine.

This is it.

There's never going to be a better moment.

Ever.

"Liam," I say. His name suddenly sounds foreign on my tongue, the way it does when you say a word over and over again until it ends up sounding like nonsense. "Liam," I try again, but it still sounds weird. I clear my throat.

"Yeah?" he says.

"I need . . ." I was going to say *I need to tell you something*, but that seems too dramatic, so I start over. "Liam." I take a deep breath. "I like you."

That's what I say. *I like you.* The moment is perfect and beautiful and I've rehearsed it a million times in my mind, how I would say all these amazing things about him and our friendship and how I've felt this way for a long time and how I've been dying to tell him but I've been too afraid. But in the moment, in this amazing perfect beautiful moment, I don't say any of that. I just say "I like you."

"You like me?" he says. And it's in that moment that I hear it in his voice. He's confused, the way you would be when someone just blurts something out like that. But there's something else, just a tiny little twinge of something, something I wouldn't have probably even noticed except for the fact that I know him so well. Panic.

Which makes *me* feel panicked. Suddenly, I want to take

it back. I want to blow it off and tell him I mean as a friend, of course, that even though he's been seeing a therapist, that I still like him, that nothing's changed, that we're still best friends. But it's too late. He knows me just as well as I know him. He would realize exactly what I was doing.

"Yes," I say, and my voice sounds surprisingly firm. "I like you. As more than a friend. I have for a while, actually." The words are tumbling out, and I force myself to keep talking, because I can feel the moment subtly shifting from amazing and perfect and beautiful to awkward and horrible and filled with regret. "And obviously this doesn't have to change anything, you know, between us, we can still, ah, be friends and everything. It's not like I'm going to be weird around you now. It's just that you shared something with me that you hadn't wanted to talk about, and so I felt like I had to share something with you. Well, not *had* to share it, I mean, I wanted to share it, so—"

"Aven," he says, cutting me off. And now there's something else in his voice. Something even worse than panic. Sympathy. "I'm . . . I mean, I'm really flattered you would say that. And I'm sorry if I gave you the wrong idea just now, talking about how I came to your hotel room instead of Izzy's."

"You didn't," I say, but it's a lie. Of course he gave me the wrong idea by saying that he came to my room instead of Izzy's! Why would Liam bring that up unless he was trying to let me know he likes me better than her? And if he likes me better than her, shouldn't that mean he likes me as more than a friend? Since Izzy was (is?) his girlfriend?

"What I meant was that it's pretty telling that I didn't want to talk to Izzy at all, that maybe it meant things with her really have run their course."

"Well, obviously, since you just broke up with her," I say, irritated.

He shakes his head and goes to reach for my hand. "Aven . . ."

But I don't want to hear it. I know what he's going to say. That he cares about me so much, that this doesn't change anything, that we can still be as close as we always have been. He'll say all those things, and maybe we will still hang out and talk just as much, but things will be different.

They just will.

Our friendship is completely and totally changed now—every time he flirts with a girl, every time he hooks up with someone, he's going to be worried about my reaction. Every time something totally innocent happens like those crab fights on the beach, he'll be wondering if he's giving me the wrong idea or sending mixed messages. He'll always be worried about how I feel.

And the thing is, he's right to be.

I don't want to be around when he meets some new girl, one he likes better than Izzy, one who wants to read the same books as him and listen to his music and stay up all night talking, one who connects with him in the same way

I do. I don't want to have to see the way he'll inevitably look at me whenever he's around that girl, with a mix of pity and sympathy.

I should have never told him.

I was building up this big reveal in my head, imagining what would happen after I told him the truth, but really, the *moment* is what I was holding on to. I *needed* that moment, needed the possibility of it being amazing and perfect the way I wanted it to be. I built it up so much that as soon as we were out here, and there was sun and palm trees and ocean and hands brushing, I thought that meant something.

But the truth is, if you like someone, and that person likes you back, you don't need some big moment. It just happens.

And I'm mad at myself for not realizing that before I went and ruined everything.

And I'm mad at Liam for trying to pretend everything can just go back to being the same.

I stand up and brush the sand off my shorts.

"Where are you going?" Liam asks. "We need to talk about this."

"No, we don't. It's fine. Remember? You said nothing had to change."

"It doesn't."

"Then why do we have to talk about it?" I glance over my shoulder down the beach, like I'm looking for someone or on my way somewhere, like suddenly I have places to be. I'm trying to be nonchalant, but of course it's not going to work. Liam knows me way too well for that.

"Aven," Liam says. "We should talk about it. I think you—"

"I don't want to talk about it," I say. "I've done enough talking about it."

"We haven't even talked about it for one second!"

"What's the point?" I say bitterly. "So you can say more bullshit things to me about how nothing's going to change, how everything can be exactly the way it's always been?"

"That's not bullshit." He stands up and goes to put his arms around me, but I push him away.

"Don't," I say. "Just . . . please . . . don't."

"Okay." He seems a little shocked by my reaction, and he holds his hands up in surrender. "But please, Aven, don't leave. You're crying."

I realize he's right. I'm crying. I don't know when I started, but I am. Tears have filled my eyes, and a salty trail is sliding down one of my cheeks.

I don't want him to see me crying.

I don't want him to know I like him.

But it's too late.

I turn around and run.

NINE

BY THE TIME I GET BACK TO MY HOTEL ROOM, my whole body is shaking with sobs. I can't stop. I've cried over Liam before—in ninth grade when he asked Kendri Robb to the freshman dance, when it became obvious he was getting serious with Izzy, when he wrote this really amazing song that was so powerful I couldn't help but be moved to tears—but it was nothing like this.

This is real crying.

The kind of crying that leaves you feeling tired and headachy, the kind of crying you can't stop or hide, the kind of crying you only do when it's caused by something real, not just your ego or a temporary hurt. This kind of crying means you risked something, you took a chance and lost something important, something you have no chance of getting back.

But even this kind of crying has to end, and after half

an hour or so, I don't have any tears left. There's a headache brewing at the back of my eyes, pricking me and threatening to turn into something major.

I go into the bathroom and spot Quinn's travel bag sitting on the sink. I paw through it until I find a tiny bottle of Advil near the bottom. I pound two pills, and then catch sight of my reflection in the mirror. I look crazed. My eyes are puffy and bloodshot, my face is splotchy, and my hair is stringy. Why would my hair be stringy from crying?

I splash water on my face and try to figure out what the hell I'm supposed to do now. This vacation has been a total disaster. I haven't even gotten to do one fun thing. No boat rides. No parasailing. No bonfires on the beach. The one time I got to swim in the ocean was because someone knocked me into the water during a crab fight.

I think about taking a shower, but the whole thing just seems like way too much effort. So instead I throw myself back down on my bed and pull the covers over my head. Maybe I'll just stay here all day. Why not? I have nowhere to be and nothing to do.

I'll just sleep. I wish I had some of those Xanax pills everyone's always taking to help them relax. I think those two friends of Quinn's, Celia and Paige, have a hookup. Maybe I should ask them for a couple of pills. Why not? I deserve to be able to relax a little.

I squeeze my eyes shut and will myself to sleep.

After about ten minutes of tossing and turning, there's a knock on the door.

Liam.

It has to be.

He's come to see if I'm okay, if I'm so heartbroken over him that I'm lying in bed crying. Ha! I mean, I am. But there's no way I'm going to let him know that.

"Go away!" I yell without moving the covers off my head. I'm not sure if the person outside can hear me, but they knock again.

And then, a female voice. "Aven? Are you in there?"

Oh.

It's Izzy. Great. Just great. I really do not want to talk to her. What if she asks why my face looks like a swollen tomato? I realize I should have just pretended I wasn't here. But now I've answered her, and so she knows I'm in the room. Ugh. I can't even hide from my friends right.

Whatever.

I get out of bed and head over to the door.

I fling it open.

"Wow," Izzy says when she sees me. "What's wrong with you?"

"Allergies."

"Allergies?" She frowns. "You don't have allergies."

"Yes, I do. To the Gulf Coast air."

"The Gulf Coast air?"

"Yeah. You know, the red tide? It's kicking up, and it got my nasal passages inflamed." We learned all about red tide a few months ago, as part of our "senior experience" class on the biosphere of the Gulf Coast. It was the school's way of making at least something about this trip educational. There was a big kerfuffle at the beginning of the year between a bunch of parents—half of them wanted our trip to have mandatory activities, like trips to the historical society and ocean walks followed by written reports. And the other group wanted it to be purely recreational, since we'd all worked so hard for the past four years.

It was actually kind of a big deal, but of course everything was decided behind closed doors in a really political kind of way. No one even asked the Student Action Committee what they thought.

"There's red tide today?" Izzy says. She pulls out her phone and starts googling. "They didn't post any warnings."

"Um, it's gone now, I think," I say. "I just have some, you know, ah, lingering effects. It was just down the beach."

"Oh." She sounds doubtful, but she puts her phone away.

"Anyway, what are you doing here?" I say. "I thought you had a headache."

"It never materialized," she says. She sits down on Quinn's bed. I hope she doesn't mess it up. Quinn will think I did it.

"Oh. Well, that's good."

"Yeah. Anyway, I wanted to say I'm sorry for just leaving you there like that, you know, at the café."

"That's okay," I say. "You weren't feeling well."

"Yeah." She takes in a deep breath. "And I hope . . . I mean, I know you were Liam's friend first and everything, but I hope we can still be friends, Aven. You mean a lot to me, and even though Liam and I are broken up, I want to make sure you and I stay friends. I don't want it to be awkward."

"Me neither."

She smiles.

I smile back. "Are you . . . I mean, are you okay?"

"Surprisingly, yes. I mean, maybe it just hasn't hit me yet, but . . . me and Liam, we were never . . . we just didn't make that much sense. I never understood him the way you do."

She gives me a look, and my heart catches in my throat. Does she know? Should I tell her? She nods at me, almost like she's giving me her permission. Or maybe I'm reading into it too much. Either way, it doesn't matter. Liam doesn't think of me as anything more than a friend, and he made that perfectly clear. So whether or not I have Izzy's blessing means nothing. I stay quiet, and after a second, the moment passes.

"Anyway," she says, "I just wanted to come and apologize."

"Okay." I wait for her to ask me what I'm doing for the rest of the day, if I want to hang out or do something. But she doesn't. She just squeezes my shoulder and then walks out the door.

And once she's gone, I realize it. Izzy and I probably won't be friends anymore. And it has nothing to do with Liam and how I feel about him. The truth is, Izzy and I were only friends because of Liam, the way people are only friends when they have something holding them together. Once that thing is gone, so is the friendship.

It's not the kind of friendship I had with Quinn and Lyla, the kind of friendship that's true and deep and built to stand the test of time. But then again, the thing I had with Quinn and Lyla didn't stand the test of time, either. And if that's true, then how can anyone's friendship survive?

The whole thing is making my head spin.

I sit down on my cot and look around the empty room. Even though everything's messy and strewn about—Quinn's shoes on the floor, Lyla's covers disheveled and hanging off the bed—the room somehow still seems lonely. It looks like it should be filled with three girls on their senior trip, laughing and talking and making plans. It's just how I feel inside, messy and empty.

My phone buzzes.

If it's that email, I'm going to throw it across the room.

But it's not. It's a text.

From Colin.

Who's Colin? Oh! The bartender from yesterday.

Hey! Just wondering if you're up for the sunset cruise tonight? It's going to be really fun. Hit me back.

I start to type back a no with some excuse about how I have plans, but then I realize just how much of a lie that would actually be—I have no plans. Absolutely none. All I have is this empty room and a broken heart.

And I'm in Florida.

I'm tempted to curl up under the covers and just go to sleep, but I know deep down that will make me feel worse.

And what's the harm in going out with a guy I met on vacation? It sounds fun. Unless, of course, he turns out to be a serial killer who wants to dump me overboard.

Hmmm.

What's your last name? I type back.

The reply comes immediately.

Wallace ☺

I do a quick google. He checks out—student at USF, server on Siesta Key.

Then I google "Siesta Key sunset cruise." There's only one, and it looks fun, kind of like a party boat but not as crazy. And it seems like the boat gets filled with a lot of people, at least according to the pictures online. So if Colin's a psycho stalker, this probably wouldn't be the kind of thing he would invite me to.

I hesitate for a second, and then, before I can change my mind, I text back.

I'm in.

A few hours later, as I'm wandering down the streets of Siesta Key, looking for the place where this sunset cruise is supposed to set sail, I'm starting to realize what a truly horrible idea this was.

First, I had no idea what, exactly, I was supposed to wear on a sunset cruise, and I was pretty sure that anything I'd brought with me was totally inappropriate. And not the good kind of inappropriate either, where you'd be walking down the street and maybe some mom with her little kids would give you a look like, *Are you seriously showing that much skin in public?* No, all my clothes were inappropriate in a *you can't wear that on a sunset cruise because people will think you're a fourth grader and kick you off the boat* kind of way.

So I spent my afternoon shopping. The shopping was actually kind of fun—there were all these cute little boutiques filled with cool things like earrings made out of shells and flowing beach wraps and starfish paintings and boat shoes. It was the perfect way to spend the day, just strolling along from store to store.

The only problem was that all the salespeople were so friendly.

In Connecticut, you're lucky if you can get someone to pay attention to you when you walk into a store, but here it was a completely different story. Not only did someone offer to help me as soon as I walked in anywhere, but they actually seemed like they cared about whether I found something I liked. A little too much, actually.

I ended up showing everything I tried on to this salesgirl, Mona, who oohed and aahed and made me feel like a model. But then she convinced me to buy this really cute chevron-print sundress because she told me it would be perfect for a sunset cruise, and of course I needed high-heeled sandals to go with it, and even though I really couldn't afford any of it, I said screw it and bought everything anyway.

I mean, it wasn't like I'd spent that much money on the trip so far—I hadn't been eating out and having fun and blowing money on stupid stuff the way I thought I'd be. So I figured it was okay to splurge a little.

Plus, I was going on a date.

A real date with a real boy on a real sunset cruise.

The only problem was that now I was about to be late and I had no idea where I was going. I had my phone out and was trying to follow google maps, but I couldn't figure out how to get it off the driving directions, which were different from the walking directions because of things like one-way streets. Not that I'd seen many one-way streets around here.

But still, there was no way these directions were right.

It said the boat was taking off from two miles away.

Two miles away? How could that be right? I thought Siesta Key was supposed to be small. And my hotel's right on the ocean. Shouldn't the boat just, you know, take off from somewhere close by? Of course, I know the ocean's big, but you'd still think—

The sound of laughter fills the street, and I turn around to see a pedicab go whizzing by. Quinn's sitting in the back with her two friends, Celia and Paige. Her hair whips back as they fly by, talking and giggling. Well. She certainly looks like she's having fun. I shake my head and marvel at the fact that I risked my place on the Student Action Committee (which, let's face it, wasn't that big of a sacrifice, but still) to make sure I got to room with Lyla and Quinn, and those two don't even care.

Nope.

They're just off gallivanting around in the back of pedicabs, their hair all shiny and flying. Okay, so Lyla wasn't there. But she's probably out somewhere, too, laughing and giggling as she juggles all the boys who want her, totally over her mini meltdown this morning.

Meanwhile, here I am, getting sweaty and muggy, my hair turning into a complete mess because I didn't realize how far I'd have to walk.

I'm never going to make it before the boat leaves.

I try to walk faster, but it's definitely not happening in these shoes.

I look around for a pedicab, but there are none. Of

course not. Quinn and her stupid friends probably took the last one.

Finally, I spot a regular cab in front of one of the hotels on the strip. A guy in a suit gets out and talks to the driver for a moment before handing him a few bills. The cabbie counts the money and then starts to pull away, but I start calling for him to stop.

"Wait, wait!" I scream. "Please, wait!"

The cabbie looks annoyed, but he pulls over next to the sidewalk where I'm standing.

"Hi," I say, leaning down so I can talk to him through the passenger-side window. My breathing is heavy, and I'm shocked to realize how totally out of shape I am. I really need to start doing some cardio. I'll have plenty of time now that I won't be hanging out with Liam and Izzy any- more. Maybe I'll get into crazy good shape and then write an e-book about my transformation and get rich off it. It will give me a chance to do some writing now that my romance novel is on the back burner.

"What can I do for you?' the cabbie asks.

"I need a ride."

He shakes his head. "Sorry, I'm an airport-only service."

I frown. "What does that mean?"

"It means I only go back and forth from the airport."

"Well, that doesn't sound like a very good business plan. You should be able to get fares on your way back to the airport if you want. Otherwise it's just a waste."

"They factor that into the price," he says.

"Yeah, but think about all the tips you're missing out on."

This seems to perk him up. Not that I can blame him—it really is a terrible business plan, only taking people back and forth to the airport. What a waste of a cab. Not to mention all the gas fumes. It's horrible for the environment.

"Anyway," I say, "uh, maybe you could take me as a fare. You know, on your way back to the airport."

"I just told you—"

"I have money!" I cry. "I'll pay double, please, it's not even that far."

He sighs again, like he can't believe he's been put in the position of possibly having to strand a girl on the side of the road.

"Where are you going?" he asks.

I rattle off the address.

"That's on the other side of the key!" he says.

"It's only two miles." I hold up my phone to show him, even though since he's a cabbie I'm sure he knows exactly where everything is around here.

"It's not on the way to the airport."

"It won't take that long." I can feel something building inside me, and I'm shocked to realize that if he says no, I might actually start crying. I've been able to keep the whole Liam thing out of my mind all day by focusing on tonight, by thinking about the fact that I was going to be spending the night on a boat with another guy. But now that it might not be happening, I can feel the wound in my heart starting to open just a little bit, like a stitch that's holding on desperately but might be under too much pressure to stay closed.

"Please," I say.

The driver sighs, and then says, "Fine. But no luggage."

"No luggage!" I say, getting in the car before he can change his mind. "I don't have any luggage!"

He looks at me. "You're sitting in front."

Oh. I hadn't realized I'd gotten into the front seat. But now that I'm in the cab, there's no way I'm getting out.

"Yeah, so?"

He shrugs and sort of widens his eyes like he can't believe he's picked up such a crazy. But five minutes later he's dropping me off in front of the dock, and I'm so relieved I can't believe it.

"Thank you, thank you, thank you," I say.

I tip him ten dollars on a five-dollar ride, and then I'm out of the car and smoothing my hair and hoping I don't look as frantic as I feel.

I spot Colin right away, standing over by the sign for Tucker's, one of the waterfront restaurants that are flanking the dock. He's wearing a burnt-orange sweater and baggy khaki shorts, and his hair is wet like he just got out of the shower. He's even cuter than I remembered, taller and more built.

"Hey," he says, smiling when he sees me.

"Sorry I'm late," I say.

"You're not late. And you look amazing."

"Thanks."

He takes my hand, and surprisingly, it doesn't feel weird. It feels almost normal, like he's not a complete stranger I met on the beach earlier, but someone I've known for a while, someone I can trust.

We start walking toward the boat.

"Have you ever gone on this cruise before?" I ask.

"A couple of times," he says. "But not since last summer. The music is usually good, and it's amazing to watch the sun set over the ocean."

"Sounds awesome," I say.

When we get to where the guy is taking people's tickets so they can board, Colin pulls two out of his pocket. "I got the tickets while I was waiting for you," he says. "I hope that's okay. Sometimes these things sell out, especially during big vacation weeks."

"Oh," I say. "That's totally fine." I fumble with the purse I'm carrying and pull out my wallet. "How much were they?"

"Don't worry about it," he says, and I blush.

The guy at the door rips our tickets in half and hands us the stubs.

"Thanks," I say, making sure to put the stub in my wallet. Who knows? This could be my first date with my future husband. I mean, how awesome would that be? That on the day Liam breaks my heart, I meet another guy, one who's sweet and amazing and pays for things and wants to marry me. I'm already thinking about how I could fit that subplot into my book.

Colin leads me up a long ramp into a back part of the boat. The boat is crowded, but not overly so. There are enough people so that it feels like a party, but not so many that you can't move.

We find a spot down by the end of the bow and stand there for a second, looking out over the water. It turns out I didn't have to worry about being late, because the boat isn't moving yet, and it doesn't even seem like anyone's in that much of a hurry to get it going.

"Are you having a nice trip so far?" Colin asks.

"Pretty nice," I say, which is obviously a complete lie. Unless you count having to room with your two ex–best friends and getting rejected by the boy you love as pretty nice.

"Uh-oh," Colin says. "Why just pretty nice? Are the frat boys of Siesta Key giving you a hard time? Did a retired golfer give you a dirty look for getting in the way of his shot? Just tell me who messed with you and I'll make sure they don't do it again."

I laugh. "No, no, everyone here's been so nice to me. It has nothing to do with the people."

"Then what does it have to do with?" He leans over the side of the railing, and his eyes are warm, and I can tell he really does want to know—he's not just asking to be nice or to make conversation. He's actually really interested in me and my trip and what I have to say.

Obviously there's no way I can tell him I'm upset over some other guy when I'm on a date with him. But I still feel like I need to say *something,* since he's being so nice to me. And besides, it might be nice to talk to a neutral third party who knows nothing about the situation.

"It's just . . . did you ever build something up in your mind so much and then realize it's not everything you thought it would be?"

He frowns. "Like realizing your parents are just people, and not these amazing humans who aren't supposed to do anything wrong?"

"Sort of," I say, "but it's more like . . . I just thought this trip was going to be amazing and wonderful and perfect and it just turned out to be a mediocre normal kind of trip."

"Well, that usually happens when you build something up in your head. And besides, you can't say this was a medio-cre normal kind of trip." He gives me a flirtatious grin. "You met me."

"True." I smile.

"Do you want something to drink?" Colin asks.

"Depends," I say. "Is it going to be as good as the drink

you made me on the beach yesterday?"

"Definitely not," he says. "But it will at least be served by me, so it'll still be special."

I laugh. "I'll have a Diet Coke."

"You got it."

Colin disappears through the thickening crowd of people, heading toward the bar. I turn around and look back out across the ocean. The sun is starting its descent, but it's still flaming red, shooting sparks of burnt orange into the sky. I take in a deep breath of tropical air, then lean down and watch the waves sliding lazily against the bottom of the boat.

A wave of vertigo passes over me, and I grab the railing to steady myself.

After a moment, my head feels better, but my brain starts moving. It's like I was okay when I was standing in one place, but now that something has shifted, my whole energy has as well.

Images and thoughts start flashing through my mind one by one.

Liam, sitting there on the beach while we played tic-tac-toe, his face serious.

The way his hair flopped over his forehead, the look in his eyes when he told me he didn't like me as anything more than a friend.

How he didn't even try to call me to see if I was okay, to

try to talk to me about what had just happened between us.

How I thought I was being so brave and smart by telling him how I felt, but it wasn't brave or smart at all. It was just stupid. Being brave is being afraid of something and doing it anyway. I *was* afraid to tell Liam, that's true—but I was more afraid of feeling this way about him and *never* telling him, of having to live with this secret for the rest of my life.

That was my biggest fear.

My mind is completely confused, the kind of confusion that can only come from a situation that has nothing to do with rules or logic but is based solely on emotion.

Before graduation, I will . . . tell the truth.

My eyes fill with tears that threaten to spill down my cheeks. I want to go back in time and tell my fourteen-year-old self that if she wants to tell the stupid truth, if she's so concerned about honesty, then maybe she should just do it herself instead of wasting four effing years banging her head against the wall before ending up in the exact same boat (ha-ha, boat!) she would have ended up in when she was fourteen.

I'm starting to get that same light-headed feeling again, so I turn away from the railing, hoping that not watching the waves will help. As I do, I catch sight of my reflection in the windows that enclose the middle part of the boat. Shit. I knew I should have never bought cheap drugstore eyeliner. I was hardly even crying and now I have black smudges under my eyes. I do my best to wipe them away with my fingers, but I can't be totally sure I got it all, so I decide to take a quick trip to the bathroom.

I start making my way back toward the other end of the boat, figuring that's the best place to start looking for the restrooms. When I finally find them, there's—predictably—a line. I sigh and think about just ditching the whole idea, but now in addition to the eyeliner situation, I actually have to go to the bathroom.

Why is there never a line for the men's room? And why can't women just use their bathroom if we need to? Like, if the men don't mind, shouldn't it be okay? I mean, I understand that it could be totally awkward if the bathroom is filled with people, but if it's empty, then—

Oh.

Is that Quinn? I can see her a few people ahead of me in line, jiggling her leg impatiently. She turns her head slightly, and when she does, I can see that she's been crying. Her face is red, and her eyeliner is even more smudged than mine is. Why is Quinn crying? And since when does she wear eyeliner?

A second later, she disappears into the bathroom. Oh, well, I tell myself. Not my business. First, I'm the last person Quinn would want to see if she's upset about something. And second, I have my own problems to deal with.

Still, I feel like maybe I should do *something*.

I scan the crowd for Quinn's friends Celia and Paige. Maybe I can send them in after Quinn to make sure she's okay. But Celia and Paige are nowhere to be found.

When I finally get into the bathroom a few minutes later, I go into a stall, pee, then wash my hands and fix my makeup. I'm on my way out when I spot Quinn's feet under one of the doors. She's still in there.

She doesn't want to talk to you, I tell myself. *She's just going to be a brat, and you'll end up feeling worse than you already do.*

But then I think about earlier today, with Lyla, how I reached out, and how she responded, and how it was the first time in a long time I'd felt any kind of connection with her. And besides, what if Quinn's really in trouble? What if something really bad happened to her? I know the chances are small, but do I really want to walk out of here without at least checking on her?

I sigh and walk toward the stall.

I give a tiny little knock on the door, halfway hoping she's not going to hear it and then I can be like, *Well, I tried, she didn't answer* and then get back to my own misery, which is more than enough to bear, thank you very much.

"Someone's in here," Quinn snaps.

I roll my eyes. Yeah, no shit. "Quinn?" I try, half hoping she'll tell me to go away. But there's just silence. "Quinn, it's Aven. Are you okay?"

"I'm fine," she says firmly.

"Okay." I think about leaving, but how can I know she's telling the truth, that she really is okay? As much as I don't want to get involved, how can I just leave her in there when she's obviously upset? "Are you sure?"

"Yeah," she says. There's a pause, and I can tell she's trying to think of something she can say to make me go away. "I'm just a little seasick."

Wow. That's not even a good lie. "Quinn," I say, sighing, "I saw you crying."

"I'm not crying!"

"You were when you came in here. I saw you."

"No, you didn't, because I wasn't crying." Okay, now she's just being insulting. I mean, seriously, how can she think I'm going to buy her bullshit that easily? Then she sniffs! The girl tells me she's not crying and then she *sniffs*. Wow.

"You're still crying!" I say, mad now. I start pounding on the stall door. "Let me in!"

"No!" she says. "I'm going to the bathroom."

Right. Like I'm really going to be believe anything she says now. I take a step to the side and then lean down so I can peer under the door. She's just sitting there crying, not looking seasick at all. "You are not going to the bathroom," I say. "And you don't seem seasick."

"Oh, for the love of God," she says, reaching out and unlocking the door.

I straighten up and shuffle into the stall with her.

Wow. It's close quarters in here.

"If you think we're going to have some big bonding moment in here, then I'm sorry to disappoint you, but I'm not in the mood."

I don't even have it in me to try and pretend to be offended. She just seems kind of pathetic, with her eyes all red from crying and this whole false bravado thing she's doing, where she tries to act like she doesn't care about me being in here when it's so obvious she needs a friend.

"Oh, Quinn," I say, reaching over and grabbing some toilet paper off the roll. I hand it to her. "Blow your nose."

She does it grudgingly.

I reach into my purse and pull out a tiny can of Sprite that's left over from when I got them for me and Lyla earlier. What is up with me helping everyone through their meltdowns? I'm such a good friend. You'd think people would take the idea of us all making up a little more seriously.

"Here," I say, popping the top. "Drink."

Quinn wrinkles her nose. "I'm not drinking in a bathroom stall."

"Knock it off, Quinn, it's not contaminated." Seriously. This is not the time to be worried about germs.

She reaches out and takes the soda from me and has a slow sip. "Thanks," she says after a moment.

"Feel better?" I ask.

She thinks about it. "Actually, I kind of do."

I nod in satisfaction, then take the can back from her and take my own sip. "So why are you hiding in the bathroom?" I ask. I know I thought I didn't really want to get involved, and I'm still not sure I do, but I'm also dying to know what's going on. Quinn's not the type to show her emotions like that, to get all riled up and start freaking out in some random bathroom. She's always been quiet and steady, never veering from her chosen path, always doing well in school and doing the right things.

"Why do you care?" she snaps, her moment of vulnerability obviously having passed.

I think about lying, about telling her I don't care, but then I think, what the hell? The worst has already happened—I've already told Liam how I feel and gotten rejected—what do I really have to lose by telling Quinn how much I miss her?

"Quinn . . ." I start, thinking about where to begin, what to say, how to let her know I still care about her, that I think about her a lot, that sometimes I miss her so much it feels like a physical ache.

"Stop," she says, before I can figure out where to start. "I can't . . ."

I nod, letting her know that I understand she's upset and can't deal with having any more emotion piled onto her right now. I'm not even hurt—I know it's not personal. I kneel down in the stall so that I'm eye level with her. "You want to talk about it?"

She shakes her head no, but a second later she says, "It's a boy."

God, what is it with this place? I'm all upset about a boy, Lyla was all upset about a boy, and now Quinn's crying in the bathroom because of a boy. "Oh." I nod in understanding. "He broke your heart?"

"I don't know," she says. "I just met him. And he seems . . . I mean, it seems like maybe he likes me."

"So then what's the problem?" Sounds perfect to me. He likes her, she likes him. What is she complaining about?

"The problem is that we're all wrong for each other. And he lives here. And I hardly know him."

I shrug. "The heart wants what it wants." I mean, seriously, what is wrong with her? A guy she likes likes her back, and she's upset because he's all wrong for her and lives far away? Has she never heard of planes, trains, automobiles, and FaceTime? And what does that even mean, that they're all wrong for each other? How can they be all wrong for each other if they really like each other? Hasn't she watched any romantic comedy, like, ever? The people who are the most wrong for each other are actually the ones who might be the most right.

"Yeah, well, what if the heart is really messed up and confused?"

"All hearts are messed up and confused."

"So then how can I trust what's real and what isn't?"

I shake my head. "You can't."

"You're making no sense," she says, sounding frustrated.

There's a knock on the stall door. "Come on!" a voice yells. "There are people waiting out here! Find somewhere else to do that lesbian shit."

I sigh and then stand up. I want to help her, but I just . . . I don't know if I can. I'm jealous of her. She's found someone she likes, who might like her back, and she's getting caught up in all the wrong things, like how to know if it's right or if she can trust her heart. No one's heart can be trusted, that's why it's your heart and not your brain. But even though I know it might be a lost cause, I find myself turning around.

"Quinn, if you've found someone you really like, and he likes you back . . . well, that's amazing. He must be pretty special if he's making you react like this. And I know we're not friends anymore, and you don't know what's going on in my life. But you need to trust me when I tell you this—if you think you have a chance with someone you really like, well, then you need to follow your heart. That, I know."

I reach out and squeeze her shoulder, and then I turn and walk out of the stall.

Follow your heart.

It seems so easy.

Just three little words.

Three little words with the power to make you

ridiculously happy, or make you feel like everything's a total mess.

When I get back to the place to where I left Colin, he's standing there holding two plastic cups filled with soda.

"Hey," he says when he sees me. "There you are. I was starting to think maybe you'd left me."

"Never," I say. "I was just, um, talking to a friend." I take the drink he's holding out, and I'm surprised to find that my hand is shaking a little bit.

"Is everything okay?" he asks. "You seem a little upset."

"Oh, I'm fine," I say. "It's just that my friend was having a hard time. She was crying in the bathroom."

"Is she okay?" His eyes fill with concern. "Does she want to hang out with us?"

"Oh, no, she's fine. I mean, she will be. She was just worried about some guy."

"Ahh." He nods, like he knows all about girls getting upset about some guy. "Let me guess, she likes someone who doesn't like her back?"

"No, the opposite actually. She likes someone who does like her back."

He shakes his head. "So then what's the problem?"

"The problem is that she thinks he's all wrong for her."

He takes a sip of his drink and leans over the side of the

boat. "Girls make everything so complicated."

I'm about to call him out for being sexist, but he quickly adds, "I mean, guys can, too, don't get me wrong. But to me, it's simple. If you like someone and they like you back, it should work. It shouldn't be hard or awful or cause you to run into the bathroom crying. You know what I mean?"

"Yeah." I take a sip of my drink and lean against the railing next to him, making sure not to look down. At that moment, the boat starts inching away from the dock, slowly and smoothly making its way into the water. A cheer goes up from the crowd.

Colin turns and puts his arm around me, pulling me close. I lean into him, enjoying how strong and sturdy his body feels after I've felt like I was spinning all day.

But he's not Liam.

No one's Liam.

And I can't change the way my heart feels.

And right now, my heart isn't here.

It's back on that beach, with Liam, still thinking about the way he looked when I told him how I felt—the surprise, the confusion, the sympathy. My mind feels sharp, like I'm seeing every single detail too clearly, too bright, too defined. I don't like it. Suddenly, I want something to dull the memory.

"Hey," I say, turning my face toward Colin. "Do you know where there's alcohol?"

It's a dumb question, of course, because Colin's a college student. Of course he knows where there's alcohol. Or at least, he knows who on the boat has it.

He takes off and returns a few minutes later with a plastic cup that looks identical to the Diet Coke I just finished, but Colin promises me that this one has rum in it.

"Wow," he says as I take a long gulp. "Be careful. We can get you more."

The vibe on the boat has changed, or at least, it has in my mind. Everyone seems happier now that we're out on the water. The music starts, and it's loud with a strong rhythm, the kind of music you can feel as it beats in your chest.

"I want to dance," I say to Colin.

He grins. "Really? I didn't peg you for a dancer."

"You shouldn't try to peg me," I say as I take his hand and lead him toward the dance floor. "That's a mistake. I'm unpeggable."

I know I'm making no sense, but I don't care. The alcohol has already started to dull the pain in my brain, and it's making everything else a little fuzzy, too—the way Colin's hand feels in mine, the bodies around us as I throw myself into the mix.

We dance.

And dance.

And dance.

I drink.

And drink.

And drink.

Not enough to get crazy drunk—I keep myself on the stronger side of buzzed, just enough so that everything feels warm and good and safe. We spend all night on the dance floor, all night in a mix of sweaty bodies and pulsing music and blurred feelings.

When the boat begins to pull into the harbor and the music stops and the lights go on, panic sears through my body. The dancing and partying was my escape. And now that's over.

"Come back to my room," I whisper in Colin's ear.

He shakes his head. "You're drunk."

"I'm not drunk," I say. "I'm a little buzzed, but I'm not drunk."

I can tell he wants to, but he's afraid he's going to be taking advantage of me. Which he's not. The ship has completely stopped now, and people are starting to move toward the exit, creating a bottleneck that keeps us locked in place for a few minutes. But even so, I can tell that my buzz is already fading, that my mood was as much because of the music and the dancing and the boat as it was about the alcohol.

Sure enough, once we're on the sidewalk and the cool night air hits my face, I'm back to feeling almost completely normal. I immediately wish I were back on the boat, another rum and Coke in my hand, that feeling of reckless abandon coursing through my veins. It's a little disconcerting, actually, the fact that I'm using alcohol to dull my pain. Am I becoming an alcoholic? Is telling Liam how I felt going to be my undoing? Am I spiraling down into the seedy world of addiction?

"I'm fine," I say out loud, more to myself than to Colin, who hasn't even asked me if I'm okay.

He looks at me, confused. "Okay," he says.

"I'm serious," I say. "I'm not drunk."

"Still," he says. "I'll walk you home."

"Okay." This seems like a good idea, even though my desire to take him back to my room has cooled off a little. It's almost like a dream or something, where you wake up and kind of go, *Wow, what was I thinking?* But maybe I'm just having cold feet about hooking up with him.

I glance at him out of the corner of my eye as we turn the corner onto Ocean Boulevard. He has a nice profile. Straight nose, full lips, manly but not too manly. Broad shoulders. Good walk, smooth and confident.

"Are you sure you're okay?" he asks.

"Yes," I say. "The air feels good."

"Okay."

We lapse into silence then. I know I'm probably supposed to ask him about school, or if he has any brothers and sisters or something. But honestly, I could care less about making small talk. I don't want to get to know someone new.

I want to be with Liam. Liam, who I already know. Liam, who knows everything about me, like how I don't like elevators because I'm afraid I'm going to get stuck, how I hate spicy food and the word "moist." Liam, who can talk to me about everything from gender roles to wars to the importance of books with pink covers.

I don't want small talk.

I want real connection.

And I don't want to make a *new* connection with someone. I want the connection I already have.

"So you're going back home tomorrow?" Colin asks. "To Connecticut?"

"The day after," I say.

He nods. "Are you excited to be graduating?"

"Yes," I say, because it's what people expect. The truth is, I'm not that excited to graduate. I like living at home. I like my parents. And once everyone goes off to college, all the possibilities will be gone. The possibility of being with Liam. The possibility that Lyla and Quinn and I will be friends again.

Everyone will go to college, and it will be like our high school relationships never even happened. Everyone will form new friendships, fall into new romances, meet new people. And then when college is over, everyone will leave again. It's actually really depressing when you think about it.

"Yeah, college is much different from high school," Colin says. "It's just so much better."

"How so?" I ask.

"Just having more control. You're not spending all day in class, learning things you're not excited about. Yes, it can be a lot of work, but it's a lot more interesting and there's more chance for self-direction."

"That's good," I say. That's the best he can come up with? Everyone knows you get more control of your schedule in college. If it were Liam, he would have said something about—ahhh! I need to stop thinking about Liam! Colin is perfectly nice. He's even putting up with the fact that I'm being kind of bratty right now, giving him one-word answers and thinking mean thoughts about him. I'm sure he has tons of good qualities, even better than Liam.

I glance over at him again.

"How tall are you, anyway?" I ask.

A look of surprise and confusion passes across his face, but he recovers quickly. "Six-two. Why?"

Ha! Liam is only six feet! And everyone knows being taller is better. It's, like, scientifically proven. Men who are taller get further in business and life. It's a known thing. Score one for Colin!

It somehow makes me feel better, this little game. I try to think of other things that might make Colin better than Liam.

"What was your GPA in high school?" I ask.

"Three point seven."

Ha! Liam's is only a 3.0! Colin is smarter than Liam!

"What was the last book you read?"

"Probably my astronomy textbook."

"No, I mean, like, for fun." Maybe if it sounds interesting, we can start a new book club. One with books I actually want to read.

"I don't read much," Colin says. "When you're in college, you don't have much time for pleasure reading."

I frown. I don't get it. How can you not have time for pleasure reading? That's like saying you don't have time to eat or brush your teeth. If Colin has time to go to parties or sunset cruises or the dining hall or . . . I don't know, *anywhere*, he should have time to read. I would much rather read than go out to some stupid frat party where a bunch of Neanderthal guys are going to be playing beer pong and doing keg stands. In fact, I would much rather read than do almost anything else. In fact, I wish I were curled up in bed with a book right now. But not in my hotel room. Back in my own bed, at home, before any of this happened. Before I told Liam how I felt.

"Oh," I say, because I realize I haven't replied and I don't know what else to say.

"Are you feeling okay?" Colin asks. He shakes his head. "I knew I shouldn't have given you those drinks."

"You didn't *give* them to me," I say, irritated. "I'm a grown woman; I'm in charge of myself." It's true, even though I don't really feel like a grown woman who's in charge of herself. In fact, I feel a little bit out of control.

Before graduation, I will . . . tell the truth.

I can't believe I did that.

I can't believe I told him.

"Did I do something wrong?" Colin asks. "You seem annoyed with me."

"No." I shake my head, feeling guilty that I've made him feel bad. It's not his fault I did something totally crazy and listened to a stupid email I sent myself when I was only fourteen. It's not his fault Liam doesn't love me.

In fact, Colin's been nothing but nice to me all night. And shouldn't that count for something? Isn't that the premise of, like, tons of romantic movies? That maybe the guy who's nice is the one you should be with, not the one you're in love with but who doesn't love you back?

Of course, there are also tons of movies where the guy who didn't want the girl in the beginning suddenly comes to his senses and becomes willing to change everything about his life and stop being a player because he's found the one girl who's worth it. Those movies are way more popular than the ones where the girl ends up with the boring nice guy.

But obviously that's because the bad-boy movies are totally unrealistic. I can't think of one real-world example where some guy has come to his senses and decided he wanted to be with a girl who'd been pining away for him for ages. On the other hand, I can think of tons of examples where a girl has wasted tons of time on some guy who didn't want anything to do with her.

"Okay," Colin says.

"I'm sorry," I say. "I just . . ." I trail off, not sure what kind of explanation to give him. Something tells me *I'm upset about some other guy who rejected me* isn't going to really go over that well. So I decide to borrow a page from Quinn's book. "I think I was just a little seasick. You know, from being on the boat and dancing and everything. But I'm starting to feel better."

"Oh, you poor thing," Colin says. "You should have told me. Wait here."

He ducks into one of the souvenir shops and reappears a moment later, holding a bottle of water.

"Thanks," I say, taking a sip.

"No problem," he says.

We continue walking up the strip, and I force myself to ask him questions about his family, how many brothers and sisters he has (two brothers, one younger, one older), if his parents are still together (yes), what he's hoping to do after school (maybe get his MBA, because he's interested in business, but he's worried about becoming a Wall Street suit, so he's not sure if that's going to be his path).

By the time we get back to the hotel, I'm starting to feel

a lot better. I've gone from thinking about Liam and being sad to actually being upset that I gave him the power to make me so upset. Here I am, out on a date with a super-nice, supercute guy, and instead of just enjoying myself, I'm worried about some stupid jerk who can't even be bothered to send me a text to make sure I'm okay after I poured my heart out to him. Seriously, we've been friends for four years, and he had to have known I was upset. And he couldn't even be bothered to text me? I mean, wow.

That was it. I was done with Liam. Liam was nothing to me.

I was onto Colin now.

I glance at him out of the corner of my eye again, wondering how far I'm willing to take my new plan. I want to kiss him. I want to kiss him badly, not only because he's cute and nice, but because I'm desperate for some other feeling, something that's going to distract me from what I'm feeling about Liam.

"Let's do something else," I say, desperate not to be left alone in my room all night. My body, which had felt kind of sluggish and depressed all day, now feels alive and almost tense, like I'm on alert and waiting for something to unleash me.

"Okay," Colin says. "What do you want to do?"

"Something fun," I say. "Maybe we could go walk on the beach. Or we could go up to my room." I grab his hand and pull him up the cobblestone sidewalk toward the front doors of my hotel. I'm not sure if Quinn and Lyla are in my room, but really, honestly, who cares? Lyla had her boyfriend spend the night. Why can't I have a boy come up to our room, too?

I'll kick them out. I'll say, "Sorry, girls, but you two need to leave this room immediately." And if they refuse, I'll just make it really uncomfortable for the two of them until they finally get the message. The mental picture of it is making me giggle, and I pull on Colin's hand harder, and he laughs as we stumble up the front walk together.

"Now, listen," I start to explain to him. "I have these roommates, and they're not—"

"Aven?" a voice calls.

I turn.

Liam.

It's Liam. He's sitting on the wrought-iron bench in front of the hotel, and he frowns when he sees me holding on to Colin's hand. I see the confusion on Liam's face as he tries to process what's happening. Not that it's that difficult—it's late at night, and I'm giggling like a crazy person and holding the hand of a random guy as I lead him toward the hotel I'm staying at. It's pretty obvious what I'm doing.

"Liam," I say, raising my chin in the air and dragging Colin forward. If Liam thinks he has any right to give me a hard time about what I'm about to do, then he's wrong. I'm not listening to Liam. La, la, la, erasing him from my mind.

I quicken my pace and keep pulling Colin toward the door.

"Aven!" Liam says, following us. His legs are longer than mine, and he's faster, and he's not trying to pull a six-foot-two college boy behind him, so he catches up to me and Colin pretty quickly. Liam steps in front of the automatic doors that lead to the hotel lobby.

"What?" I ask.

"What are you doing?" he asks, looking back and forth from me to Colin.

"What does it look like I'm doing?" I ask. "I'm going up to my room to have sex with Colin."

Colin gasps. "Whoa," he says, dropping my hand and backing a step away. "Who said anything about having sex?"

"Really, Colin?" I ask, annoyed. "What did you think we were going to be doing up in my room, playing backgammon?" It's kind of a funny thing to say, because I've never played backgammon in my life, and honestly I don't even know anyone who does. I must be under a tremendous amount of mental stress if I'm talking about backgammon.

"No, but I didn't think we were going to have sex," Colin says, totally serious, proving that he doesn't get my sense of humor at all. I wasn't *really* saying we were going to be playing backgammon.

"I didn't mean we were really going to be playing backgammon, Colin," I say, annoyed. "It was just a sarcastic remark."

"Look, I don't want any trouble," Colin says to Liam. "I just met her yesterday."

"There isn't going to be any trouble," I say. "Why would there be trouble?"

"Because your boyfriend looks like he wants to beat my ass."

I turn and look at Liam. He does kind of look like he wants to beat Colin's ass. His eyes are intense and angry, his gaze boring into Colin like he's one step away from punching him in the face. It's kind of sexy, if you want to know the truth. Not that I want anyone to actually get in a fight, but it's kind of nice knowing that Liam feels that protective of me.

Then I remember he has no right to be protective of me, that he rejected me, that it's none of his business if I'm taking Colin up to my room to have sex.

"He's not my boyfriend," I say to Colin.

"Oh," Colin says. He takes a small step back toward me, but I can tell that now he's wondering if maybe I'm crazy. He's also not sure if Liam really is my boyfriend and I'm lying about it, or if Liam is just some kind of psycho stalker. Either way you can tell he's not that psyched to get involved in the whole situation.

"He's not anything," I say.

"Oh, really?" Liam says in disbelief. "I'm not anything, huh?"

"No," I say, thrusting my chin into the air and daring him

to contradict me. "You're not." I'm suddenly aware of how close he is to me, so close I can see the flecks in his blue eyes, the tiny birthmark he has on his collarbone, the little cracks in the letters of his T-shirt from where the ink has worn away.

"So that's how it is now? After four years, it just doesn't mean anything?"

"No," I say, "it doesn't. If it did, you would have texted me earlier."

"I would have texted you earlier?" he repeats. "Jesus, Aven, it's been, like, a day."

"Yes!" I say. "A whole day! A whole day after I poured my heart out to you and you rejected me and I was left just waiting to hear from you."

"It doesn't look like you were just sitting around," Liam says, looking over at Colin again, anger flashing in his dark eyes.

"Look, Aven, maybe you should just call me later," Colin says. But it's the kind of thing you say when you don't really mean it but feel like you have to say *something*, because you want to get out of there and don't know how else to do it.

Wow. What a traitor. Just when things get a little rough, he takes off. Typical guy.

"Whatever," I say. "Go ahead." I flick my hand at him, and he takes off down the cobblestone walk.

"Well, I hope you're happy," I say to Liam. "You just ruined my night."

"Oh, yeah, sorry I ruined your random hookup with some college douche bag."

"He wasn't a douche bag!" I say. "He was nice."

"Oh, yeah, he was so nice that he came back to the hotel room of a girl he barely knew, and then as soon as he saw me, he beat a hasty retreat out of here." He shakes his head. "Asshole."

"It wasn't like that!" I say. Why am I even standing here trying to explain this to him? It's pointless. And it's none of his business. He has no right to pass judgment on my life or my decisions. If I want to hook up with a hundred douche bags, well, then, that's my prerogative. "It's none of your business," I say. "You can't stand there and judge me. You have no right."

I go to move by him, but he steps in front of me again, blocking my path. "I have no right? Aven, you told me you had feelings for me, and then a few hours later you show up with some other guy, ready to do God knows what. So yeah, it is kind of my business."

"Yeah, I told you I had feelings for you, and then you ignored me all day! You didn't even text me to see how I was doing. And now you're showing up here, trying to pretend like you have a say in what's going on in my life. When the truth is, Liam, you don't. Not when it comes to this. You lost that right when you told me you didn't feel the same way. You're not my boyfriend, Liam."

It feels like a lot of words to say at once, and I take a breath and wait for him to fire back. My voice is angry, raised. A couple of people walking into the hotel are looking at us, giving us that look that adults give teenagers when they see us showing emotion, that look that we're just being dramatic, that none of it really matters, when it feels to us, to me, like it's the only thing that matters.

"You hardly gave me any time to respond!" he says. "You just sprung everything on me and then you took off."

"Sprung everything on you?" I rage. "This has been going on for four years, Liam. You really expect me to believe you had no idea?"

"I had no idea!" he says. "How was I supposed to know?"

"Oh, I don't know," I say. "Maybe because I haven't dated anyone seriously since I've known you. Maybe because I've spent every single second of my free time with you. Maybe because I read your stupid books that I have no interest in just because I want to discuss them with you!" God, how dense can he really be?

"I'm not a mind reader, Aven," he says. "You never tried anything, you never told me how you felt."

"I shouldn't have had to!" I say. "You should have known from the way I was acting." I cross my arms over my chest, defensive. "And besides, there was never a good time."

"Really?" He laughs then, a high, sarcastic little laugh, the kind of laugh you use when you think the other person is really trying to sling bullshit at you. "There was never a good time? We only hung out, oh, I don't know, every single night!"

"Oh, yeah, right, every single night while you were dating Izzy."

"Izzy and I were dating for six months," he says. "What about the other three and a half years?"

"You had other girlfriends," I say vaguely. Which is true. Liam has had a couple of other girlfriends, Shani Peters and Jordan Block and a few other girls he'd randomly hook up with at parties.

"I didn't, and you know it!" he says. He takes a step toward me and shakes his head. "Look, I don't want to fight with you."

"Then why are you?"

"I don't know." He reaches out and takes my hand, and his touch sends electricity through my entire body. An ache fills me, a need so intense I'm not sure I'll be able to hide it from him. It's different from the way I used to feel when he touched me before—this time, I can feel that shift. Something's different—this isn't the way it used to feel when his hand would brush against mine when he handed me a soda, or even the way it was earlier when we were having crab fights in the ocean. This is different, because it's the first time he's touching me after he knows how I feel.

"Aven," he says. "I just . . . I want to talk about this."

"So talk." My voice catches in my throat, because I *don't* want to talk about this, I don't want to hear the same things over and over again about how he doesn't feel the same way. I just want things to go back to the way they were, before I told him any of it.

I'm staring down at the pavement, and he's still holding my hand, and I can see the tiny little cracks in all the cobblestones, and I get this overwhelming feeling of melancholy. It's so corny and melodramatic, but it's like those cobblestones are a metaphor—they're so beautiful, but they have all those tiny little cracks in them that you can't see unless you get so close, and it's so awful that I can hardly take it.

"Aven," Liam says. "Please, look at me."

I can't. It's like trying to lift a fifty-pound dumbbell over your head when you haven't worked out in months. But somehow, I do it. "Please," I say, and I can hear the pleading in my voice and I hate myself for it. "Can we please just go back to the way it was? Can we just pretend it never happened? Nothing has to change. You said so yourself back on the beach."

He blinks, slowly, his eyelids closing and then opening, and I can't tell if it's just that everything seems like it's happening in slow motion or if he's just blinking so slow because he's thinking, and then he lets out a long sigh. "You know we can't really do that."

"Sure we can," I say, the pleading in my voice turning to franticness. "We can just pretend it never happened. We can go back to our book club, we can just be friends again, it doesn't have to mean anything."

"It means everything." His voice is low, smoky, in a tone I've never heard him use before. "Aven, you're my best friend. And I just don't think that we're . . . I don't want to ruin that."

The words are sharp little knives stabbing my heart, over and over again. "Then let's just go back to how it was," I say.

"I just need some time to think about things," he says. "But I want you to know that I—"

I pull my hand from his. "Stop," I say. "Please, just stop." I'm crying, the tears running down my face, and I'm embarrassed and humiliated and rejected and alone. All the horrible feelings you could feel, all rolled up into one. "Please. Just. Stop."

And then I turn around and walk away, leaving him standing there.

He calls my name.

I don't turn back.

But I let myself have one last moment of wishing, one last moment of imagining that maybe things could be different. One last second where I hope maybe he'll follow me, or call after me again and beg me not to go. I want him to say my name, to tell me it's going to be okay, that no matter what we're always going to be friends, that we *can* go back to the way things were.

But he doesn't.

He lets me go.

And I wish I could do the same, that I could let go of the way I feel about him. But he's imprinted on my heart in a way that makes that impossible.

I'm not proud of what I do next, but as soon as I step off the elevator onto the second floor, I text Colin. I apologize for what happened, tell him I'd like a chance to explain, and then I *invite him to come back.*

I know apologizing is the right thing to do, so that part's fine. But the only reason I'm inviting Colin to come back is because I don't want to be alone. I can't take the thought of going back to my room, lying on my cot, tossing and turning and trying to fall asleep. It's too depressing.

I pace up and down the corridor, waiting for Colin to text me back, feeling like I'm holding on to my sanity by a thread. When I get to the end of the hallway for the second time, I press my head against the wall, trying to feel anything except the aching sadness that's permeating my body.

I start to cry. Big, ugly sobs that start deep in my chest, deep in my soul, and pour out of me. I feel out of control, both emotionally and physically. It's about Liam, most of it, anyway, but it's also just this overwhelming loneliness that I don't know how to deal with.

I'm *so* lonely.

I'm on this amazing trip, and I have no one to share it with.

My heart is broken, and I have no one to talk to.

I had all these stupid ideas for this trip—that maybe Lyla and Quinn and I would become friends again, that maybe something might happen between me and Liam.

It was all so stupid and naive—did I really think that four days could change my life forever? The only thing the last two days did was make things worse—Lyla and Quinn still hate me, things with Liam are completely screwed up, and I'm spending the night alone. It's the worst vacation I've ever had, times about a billion.

I wish I could blame it all on my fourteen-year-old self, the girl who stood on a beach with her friends and made a promise to herself, thinking that four years would be more than enough time to make that promise come true. But I can't. Because my three-days-ago self was just as bad. I thought I could change things during this trip, that I could make my life better. But the truth is, I haven't accomplished anything.

I pull my phone out and look at the screen, but Colin hasn't texted me back. I try to tell myself he's walking home and so he probably didn't hear his phone, but I know that's not true. He's not texting me back because he doesn't want to get involved with me. He thinks I'm crazy. Not that I can blame him. I mean, I spent all night drinking and dancing like an insane person, then got into a fight with another guy right in front of him. No wonder Colin doesn't want anything to do with me—he thought I was this fun, exciting girl, and all I am is a mess. A complete and total mess.

I sit there for a while, on the floor at the end of the hallway, just feeling sorry for myself. I'm all alone, because most of my classmates are out and about, having fun on their vacation. No one is just sitting around the hotel, like some kind of loser.

Except me.

After a while, I pick myself up and drag myself back to my room.

I stand outside the door for a moment, wondering again how I could be so clueless and naive to think that sharing a room with Lyla and Quinn for a few days would be enough to mend our friendship. The wounds between Lyla and Quinn and me go deep. Much deeper than one weekend is going to fix.

In fact, I'm starting to think that the rifts in my relationships—the one with Liam, the one with Lyla and Quinn—may not be able to be fixed at all.

TEN

I'VE ALWAYS THOUGHT THAT THE FIGHT WITH Quinn and Lyla was my fault. I know, logically, that that's not really true—the situation was complicated, and everyone contributed to it. But still, some part of me, the biggest part, has always felt that everything that happened was because of me. Not because I think I did anything wrong, but because if it wasn't for me, the whole situation never would have happened.

It started off innocently enough—a trip to the mall with Lyla. I don't remember why Quinn wasn't there. She might have been busy with one of the extracurriculars she was always signing up for (Quinn wanted to go to Stanford more than anything in the world, and she knew that even though her parents were both legacies and her grades were stellar, it was still going to be hard—so she was always volunteering or signing up for different clubs and activities that she thought would look good on her transcript).

Anyway, Lyla and I had been at the mall, trying on clothes in an effort to find the perfect casual T-shirt—the kind of T-shirt you could wear on a date and not feel like you were underdressed, but was also comfortable enough for hanging around the house binge watching *Scandal*.

It was so exhausting that we ended up at IHOP, sharing pancakes covered with strawberries and whipped cream, eating ourselves into a sugar coma.

"My dad asked me to move with him to New Hampshire," Lyla said when we were halfway through our stack, totally matter-of-factly, like it wasn't some big revelation.

"Oh," I said, remembering thinking that I should choose my words carefully. I knew Lyla's parents were getting divorced. She'd told Quinn and me earlier that week, and she'd said she wasn't upset about it.

Lyla's parents had always had a weird relationship—when you were at their house, you could feel it. Her dad was never really around—he's a doctor and worked a lot—and you could feel the tension in the house when he was. It wasn't necessarily uncomfortable or anything, it was just different. Kind of like when you had a guest over and everyone was trying to be on their best behavior. But of course Lyla's dad wasn't a guest—he was her dad. He lived there.

The whole vibe could be really weird, which was why we never spent much time at Lyla's house. It was, like, a known thing, even though she didn't talk about it much. So when she said she was fine with her parents getting divorced, and then acted like everything was totally normal, Quinn and I had no choice but to believe her.

But when Lyla announced her dad had asked her to move in with him, I remember wishing Quinn was there, because she always knew what to say in those situations. I was the peacemaker, I could make light of things, but Quinn—she knew what to say when people said something that might be upsetting or complicated. She would know the exact line to straddle, hitting that perfect balance between making the person feel like it was going to be okay and making sure not to discount the way they were feeling.

I was so afraid of saying the wrong thing that I hardly said anything—obviously I didn't want Lyla to move to New Hampshire with her dad. But I also didn't want her to think that if she wanted to go, there was something wrong with that.

Of course, I knew deep down she would never *really* go. Lyla and her dad weren't even close—why would she uproot her whole life, leave her mom, her school, her friends, just to start over in a new place? It didn't make sense. But the fact that she was even bringing it up as a possibility made me think she was more upset about the fact that her dad was leaving than she'd previously let on.

So all I ended up saying was, "That's interesting. Are you going to go?"

And she said she didn't know, and then we dropped it. I don't remember her asking me not to tell anyone, although later, she would insist that she did. To this day, I'm not sure who was right. All I know is that we both remember it very differently.

The three of us had plans to sleep at Quinn's house that night, so I figured we'd talk about it more then. But on the way out of the restaurant, Lyla begged off, saying she wanted to spend time at home, that she didn't want to leave her mom all alone. I should have pressed her on it. I should have asked her what she meant, I should have brought up the fact that she'd said she and her mom were fine with the split, that it was the best thing for everyone involved. I should have asked her what was really going on. I should have talked to her more. But again, I was so afraid of saying the wrong thing that I just said nothing at all.

When I got to Quinn's, we ordered pizza and talked about this new development.

"We have to support her," Quinn said. "If she wants to go to New Hampshire, we have to be there for her."

"What if she makes new friends?" I'd asked.

"Of course she'll make new friends," Quinn said. "But they won't be friends like us."

We decided we'd be the best friends ever—we'd help Lyla pack if she needed us to, we'd take buses out to see her every weekend until one of us got our license. (And a car—the thing about turning sixteen was that it was actually really easy to get a license—you just needed to go down and pass the test. Getting access to a car was the tricky part.)

We'd make sure we didn't fall out of touch or drift apart the way people always promised not to and then did anyway. We were different. We'd make an effort. We *decided*. And back then, I was naive enough to think that if you wanted something bad enough, you could make it happen.

I didn't hear from Lyla all weekend, and it made me nervous. The three of us were never out of contact with each other for that long, having a running group text that went back for months and never had more than a couple of hours of blank space.

I asked Quinn what we should do, and she said to wait until Monday, that maybe Lyla was just processing things.

So we waited for her outside school on Monday morning.

"Yo," I said when I saw her walking up from the bus circle. "Where you been?" I was trying to come off as cool and unconcerned, trying to keep it casual in case Lyla had had a rough weekend.

Lyla's face was completely blank. It was a weird look, one I'd never seen on her before.

"Yeah, we were trying to get in touch with you all day yesterday," Quinn said, finally looking up from her phone. When she saw the look on Lyla's face, she got concerned. "What's wrong? What happened?"

But Lyla didn't answer. Instead, she turned to me. "How

could you tell her?" she screamed. "I told you not to tell any-
body!"

"What?" I was confused, not really knowing what she
was talking about. Tell who? About what? She definitely
couldn't have meant telling Quinn about her dad. First of
all, Quinn already knew that Lyla's parents were getting
divorced. So it wasn't like I'd told the major part of the
secret. And second of all, Lyla, Quinn, and I told each other
everything. None of us had ever kept secrets from each other
before. It wasn't like that. Two of us weren't ever closer than
all three of us were. When it came to our friendship, we all
were the same. Best friends. Sisters.

"You told Quinn!" Lyla yelled. "What I told you about
my dad!" She was angry, angrier than I'd ever seen her.

"Lyla, I didn't think you meant Quinn! All three of us
tell each other everything." The weird thing was, even though
I was saying those words, I couldn't remember if she'd even
asked me not to tell anyone. Why would she have said that?
I wouldn't have told anyone except for Quinn, and so if Lyla
had asked me to keep the thing with her dad a secret, I felt
like I would have questioned her on it. But I wasn't going
to contradict her—not when she was looking at me like she
wanted to kill me. Seriously, it was scary. I'd never seen her
that mad at anyone before, let alone me.

"Wait, just calm down," Quinn said, shaking her head
like she was trying to make sense of everything. I let out the

breath I'd been holding, relieved. Surely now that Quinn was getting involved, everything would be taken care of. Quinn would fix it. She had to. "Lyla—"

But Lyla just seemed more upset as she turned toward Quinn. "You," she said, cutting her off. "How could you have told your mom?"

Quinn looked confused, and I did, too. Why would Quinn have told her mom about Lyla and her parents? "How did you know that?" Quinn asked.

"I know that because she told my mom! And now my mom is freaking out!" Lyla's voice had already been raised when she started talking to us, but now she was pretty much shrieking. It wasn't so much that she'd increased her volume as her tone. Her voice was so fraught with emotion that it was scary. I was nervous, and instead of trying to calm things down, I turned on Quinn.

"You told your mom?" I asked her incredulously. "Why the hell would you do that? Your mom has the biggest mouth in the world." It was true. It wasn't that Quinn's mom was a gossip, really. She wasn't the type who would call you up just to tell you the latest news she'd heard from the neighbors. It was more that she didn't have any boundaries. I'd always found Quinn's mom to be kind of cold and emotionless, so it would make sense that she wouldn't have a problem repeating things someone told her. It was like she couldn't fathom the idea that someone would want to keep secrets or try to work something out alone, in their heads.

"She does not," Quinn said. She turned to Lyla. "And I had no idea she was going to tell your mom."

"Neither one of you can keep a secret!" Lyla raged. Her hands were at her sides, her fists clenched so hard and her arms so rigid I was afraid she might be having a stroke or something. "You realize now that both my parents hate me, right?"

Obviously she was exaggerating. Why would both her parents hate her? And why was her dad offering for Lyla to come stay with him without even checking with her mom first? I understood they were going through a divorce, but really. It seemed like there was more going on than just the amicable, mutual divorce Lyla had told us about. At the very least, more was going on with *Lyla* than she wanted to let on, otherwise she wouldn't have been so upset.

"Look," I said. "We all need to calm down." The bell rang, signaling the beginning of first period. "We can talk about this at lunch. We'll blow off afternoon classes." Afternoon classes were easier to blow off because after lunch, no one really knew where you were. I knew we should get to first period, but I didn't want to just leave things the way they were until this afternoon. Lyla was way too upset. "Unless . . ." I took a deep breath. "Unless you want to go somewhere now?"

Quinn nodded immediately. "I'm in." I was glad she was

agreeing so readily, but it also made me a little bit scared. Quinn hated to miss class, so the fact that she was agreeing to skip pretty much meant she thought whatever was going on with Lyla was really serious.

We both turned and looked at Lyla.

She didn't say anything for a moment, and I held my breath. There was no way she was going to say no, was there? Obviously she was upset, and so of course she would want to go somewhere and work it out. The three of us hardly ever fought, but when we did, we worked it out immediately. It was one of the reasons our friendship had been so successful.

But Lyla shook her head. "I don't want to go," she said. "Stay out of my life."

And then she turned and walked into school.

Quinn and I sent her a group text later, asking if she wanted to talk after school. But she never replied. We thought she just needed some time. So we kept trying.

But the days of Lyla not replying to us turned into weeks. I even tried to talk to her a couple of times in the halls at school, but she wouldn't talk to me. I tried to come to her house, but her mom apologetically told me she refused to come to the door.

She never ended up going to New Hampshire. I don't know why, if she was ever really considering it, if she wanted to go or why it didn't work out.

At first, Quinn and I were a united front, bonded by

our friendship and our mission of trying to get Lyla to talk to us. But eventually, we drifted apart. I think both of us, on some level, blamed the other for what had happened—Quinn thought I should have let her know how important it was to keep Lyla's secret, or that maybe I shouldn't have even told her in the first place. And I thought Quinn should have known better than to tell her mom.

So after a while, I stopped trying to talk to either of them. Because it was just too painful.

I gave up.

ELEVEN

I DON'T SLEEP THAT NIGHT.

I can't.

I try, but it's just not working.

At around four a.m., I give up.

I slide my feet into my flip-flops, pull on my sweatshirt, and head down to the beach. I buy a coffee and a doughnut from a tiny little shop on Ocean Boulevard. I sip the coffee, and the warmth helps me to calm down, but I'm afraid the caffeine is just going to end up making me more jittery, so I force myself to take tiny sips, hoping that if I make it last, it won't give me too much of a caffeine rush.

I walk down the beach, until I'm all the way at the end, back where Liam and I sat yesterday, playing tic-tac-toe in the sand. Was that less than twenty-four hours ago? It seems like a lifetime.

I don't stay there long, turning back around and walking

until I hit the main part of the beach. I sit down and watch the sun rise, staying there until the joggers come out and the first college kids show up to get the best spots for their chairs.

I have nothing to do all day, and the time stretches in front of me like a blank canvas. Not filled with possibility, but threatening and scary. I decide to head back to my room and change into my bathing suit, maybe go for a swim in the ocean. I remember how cold it was yesterday when I fell into the water. I'm craving that kind of shock. I'm craving anything that's going to get me out of my head or make me feel anything besides this overwhelming loneliness.

But by the time I get back to my room, a feeling of exhaustion washes over me, and I can't fathom getting ready to go swimming.

Lyla's in bed, lying on her back, staring up the ceiling.

But I don't even care. Lyla being in the room is the least of my problems. I throw myself down on my cot and close my eyes. I'm not sure I'll be able to fall asleep, but I'm also too tired to move. I'm sort of nodding off, halfway between falling asleep and being awake, when the door to the room opens and Quinn walks in.

She plops down on her bed.

"Why are you guys just lying here?" she asks a second later.

"I'm sad," I say.

"I'm wrecked," Lyla says.

"Life's a mess," I say.

"I want to go home," Lyla says.

"Me too," Quinn says. "To all of the above."

We lapse into silence again, and I wonder if I should ask them what's wrong. It's the opportunity I've been waiting for, the moment where we're all together and the two of them aren't being mean or snarky. We're all upset, and it would be so easy for all of us to commiserate the way we used to. If I caught the two of them in a weak moment, they might even reply. After all, they've already confided in me a little.

But I don't say anything. My heart can't take one more disappointment.

"You know what?" Quinn asks, propping herself up on her elbow and looking at me and Lyla. "This is ridiculous."

"What is?" Lyla asks.

"That we're in Florida, and we're just sitting in this room. We should be out having adventures."

She's right—we should be having adventures, but I'm really not in the mood. I mean, I tried to have a big adventure when I got here, I tried to listen to that stupid email, and it turned into a big disaster. What's that thing they say? That the definition of insanity is doing the same thing over and over again, expecting different results? Why would I want to try to have another adventure when the first one turned out so horribly?

"Sounds exhausting," Lyla says.

"Sounds depressing," I say.

Quinn stands up, grabs a pillow off her bed, and throws it at Lyla. Then she picks up another one and throws it at me. "Get up," she says. "We're going out."

Lyla looks at her like she's an insane person who's just announced we're all going to go off our meds. "The three of us?" she asks. "Like *together*?"

There's no way Quinn can mean the three of us, together. Quinn doesn't want anything to do with us. And even if she did, there's no way Lyla would ever agree to anything like that. "Do you have anyone else to hang out with?" Quinn asks.

"No, but . . ." I can see Lyla racking her brain, looking for all the reasons it's a bad idea for the three of us to do something together.

So before she can, I say "I'm in!" and jump up off my cot. Any tiredness I was feeling earlier is gone. I know I said I wasn't going to get my hopes up when it came to the three of us, that my heart couldn't take another disappointment, but I can't help it. I've been wanting the three of us to be friends again since forever. It's an involuntary reaction.

"Me too," Lyla says. I'm shocked, but I try not to show it. The last thing I want is to scare her away. "But can I wash my face first?"

"Of course," Quinn says.

Quinn and I wait in silence while Lyla gets ready. "Okay," she says, when she emerges from the bathroom in fresh clothes. "I'm ready."

We all look at each other, waiting for one of us to tell the other two what we're going to do, or at least what the plan is. Lyla and I are looking at Quinn, since it was her idea in the first place, but she looks uncertain.

Eventually, we all just kind of shuffle out of the room and into the elevator.

On our way down to the lobby, Lyla comes up with a rule for the day.

"No talking about our fight," she says.

"And no talking about the emails we sent ourselves," I add. The two of them give me a curious look. Probably because they're not even thinking about the emails they sent themselves, and also because they probably want to know what happened with mine. But there's no way I want to talk about the disaster that happened with Liam. As much as I long to talk to them about it, I long to talk to them about it the way it used to be, the three of us so close I could tell them anything. And it's not like that anymore.

"This might be awkward," Lyla says once we're outside.

"Not any more awkward than sleeping in the same room," Quinn says. Which is obviously just to make us feel better and lure us into a false sense of security. How can hanging out be less awkward than sleeping in the same room?

We start walking, making small talk about the trip as we wander down toward the beach. Once we're on the sand, we start bending down to collect shells from the water, blending in with a group of tourists who are doing the same. I find a sand dollar, and something about the simple beauty of it makes my heart happy.

The three of us don't talk much. It's not an uncomfortable silence, it's just that we're all focused on finding the best shells. And it's actually good, as it gets us used to being around each other without actually having to talk. When our pockets are full of shells, we wander back onto Ocean Boulevard and into a cute little farmers' market that's set up on the sidewalk and overflowing into one of the municipal parking lots.

We poke around for a little while until we find these gorgeous turquoise bottles to pour our shells into. It's the perfect souvenir, and it makes me happy thinking the three of us are going to have something from this trip that's going to remind us of each other, of this moment.

"This reminds me of how we always used to buy the same things," I say. I cork my bottle and hold it up to the sun, watching the way the rays glint and reflect off the glass.

"We're not supposed to be talking about the past," Lyla says, but her voice is soft, and I can tell she's thinking about it anyway.

"You wanna get lunch?" Quinn asks, probably in an effort to change the subject. But I don't even care, because at least she's trying to prolong our time together.

She leads us to one of the open-air restaurants on the main strip, and we choose a table outside so that we can enjoy our last hours in the gorgeous Florida weather.

We can't decide what to order—everything on the menu looks amazing—so we order a bunch of appetizers and decide to share them.

It's a surreal moment—me, sitting here with Lyla and Quinn at the end of our senior trip. It's not the exact moment I had planned, but still. Hope blooms in my chest. No matter how much I try to squash it, how much I try to tell myself not to get excited, that the three of us hanging out doesn't mean anything, I still can't help but hope just a little bit.

Liam made me read a book once about the science of your brain. It said that everyone has a baseline personality and way of looking at the world that can't really be changed no matter what happens to you.

So, for example, if you're a positive person and something negative happens to you, you'll still look on the bright side. And if you tend to look at things negatively, and something good happens, you'll do your best to find something wrong with it.

So maybe this hope, this belief I have inside me that things can change and get better, is just part of who I am. Maybe trying to change it is pointless.

"Can you believe this?" I ask. "Did you ever think we'd end up sitting here together at the end of this trip?"

"No," Quinn says, her tone conveying just how unlikely she'd actually thought it was.

"No," Lyla agrees.

I take a deep breath. We're not supposed to be talking about the past. We're not supposed to be talking about the emails. It was my own rule, the one I'd come up with in the elevator on our way down here. But I just can't help myself. "I know we're not supposed to be talking about the past, and you don't have to give me any details, but . . . did you guys do what your emails said to?"

For a second, the two of them don't reply, and Quinn even looks away. I'm afraid they might think I'm crazy for bringing it up, that they're both embarrassed for me that I would even ask about those emails, since obviously only an idiot would think it was a good idea to listen to an email you sent yourself four years ago.

But then Lyla looks right at me. "Yes," she says.

"Yes," Quinn says.

I swallow. "Yes," I say, adding my voice to the chorus.

There's a small moment, a tiny opening for one of them to jump in and elaborate on what they actually did. I remember their emails just as clearly as I remember my own.

Quinn's said, *Before graduation, I promise to . . . do something crazy.*

And Lyla's said, *Before graduation, I will . . . learn to trust.*

I wonder what they did, how they grew, if listening to

their emails turned out just as horribly for them as it did for me. I wait for one of them to say something, to let the other two in, but when they stay quiet, I don't push it. I'm dying to know, but things are going relatively well, and the last thing everyone needs is for me to add pressure to the situation. So instead we make small talk and gossip about classmates as we eat our appetizers and share a cookie-dough sundae for dessert.

"We should do it again," Quinn says once the last bite of sundae is gone.

"Do what again?" Lyla asks.

"We should make more promises. Why not? We're at the beach." When we wrote those emails four years ago, we did it at the beach. We thought it was so symbolic. Silence settles over the table as we all think about it.

"Sure," Lyla says after a second. "I'm in."

I nod. "Me too."

We decide to write our promises down on real paper this time. I think now that we've all done it once, we sense just how serious it is. Promises to yourself are the most important ones you can make, and yet our fourteen-year-old selves thought an email was an okay place to put something so sacred. Now we know better.

So after we pay the bill, I duck into one of the dozens of souvenir shops and buy purple markers, green paper, and a lighter.

We walk back to the beach.

I stand there and look out at the water, taking in a deep breath of ocean air.

I press my pen into my piece of paper.

One sentence.

That's what we promised each other.

I promise to . . .

I think about what it could be, what I want for myself, for my life. Something that has nothing to do with Liam, nothing to do with Lyla and Quinn. Something I can do for myself, and not have to be dependent on anyone else.

And then, in a flash, I know exactly what to write.

I promise to . . . learn to be happy.

I fold my paper in half.

"Ready?" Quinn asks, holding up the lighter.

We all nod.

Quinn lights the papers and they fly up into the sky, burning out quicker than you would think, the flames dancing against the sky until the ashes fall, fanning out across the sand, a few of them picked up by the wind, taking off across the ocean.

The three of us stay here for a long time, just sitting on the sand, watching the sun move lower in the sky.

I know we're all thinking about the promises we made to ourselves.

There won't be an email to remind us this time.

We're going to have to remind ourselves.

* * *

That night I sleep like a baby. I think it's because of my lack of rest the night before, and the long day I spent with Lyla and Quinn. My body is exhausted, emotionally and physically.

I get woken up the next morning by the sound of Quinn stomping around our room. I sit up in bed and blink sleepily.

Quinn's standing over by the dresser, fully dressed, her suitcase next to her. "Did either one of you take my hair straightener?" she demands.

"I didn't," I say, checking my cell phone alarm. I set it last night so I wouldn't be late for the bus, but either I didn't do it right or I slept right through it.

"Because it's missing," Quinn continues. "And since I haven't used it, it had to have been one of you."

"I think it might be in the cabinet under the sink," Lyla says.

Quinn gives a big sigh, like having to go look for a hair appliance is the worst thing that's ever happened to her. She returns a moment later with the straightener and places it in her suitcase. "You guys better hurry up. You're going to be late." She turns and walks out of the room.

Well. I guess whatever peace the three of us had found yesterday is gone.

"Do you mind if I shower first?" I ask Lyla. I'm anxious to get down to the lobby, because I just realized Liam's going to be there. I'm nervous not because I want to see him, but because I'm going to have to figure out a way to *avoid* him. We're sitting right near each other on the plane—Liam, Izzy, and me. And that's definitely not good for my mental state. I'm going to have to find someone to switch seats with, which is definitely easier said than done, since everyone's already sitting with their friends.

I wonder if anyone else is in the same situation as me. I mean, there has to be someone else who's had a bunch of drama on this trip and therefore wants to change their current seating arrangements. But how do I find that person? It's not like I can just go down to the lobby carrying a sign that says, *Hey, did anyone get into a fight with their friends and want to change seats?*

"No, I don't mind," Lyla says. "Just let me wash up real quick."

She heads into the bathroom, and I grab a fresh bottle of shampoo and a pomegranate grapefruit body wash out of my suitcase. Lyla emerges a few minutes later, her hair pulled back in a ponytail, her face clean.

"See you down there," she says awkwardly as I pass by.

So much for a truce.

By the time I get down to the lobby, I have a plan. It's going to be easier to find someone who doesn't care about where they're sitting on the plane, rather than looking for some-one who actively wants to change their current seat. In other words, I need a loner.

I search the crowd, but I can't find anyone who might fit the bill. Even the kids who aren't that social have friends who are also not that social. So all the nonsocial people will be sitting together.

By the time we board the bus for the airport, I still haven't been able to change my seat. I start having flashes of Liam, Izzy, and me getting upset with each other on the plane, get-ting into some kind of fight and then getting kicked off for security reasons. They do that now—kick people off flights for security reasons, like if they're getting going and yelling about something.

But then, when we get to the airport, I spot Bruno James over by the wall. He's got his phone plugged into the socket, charging it. And I know why—it's not because his phone is dead or anything, it's because he likes to get things for free. Including the airport's electricity. He's like one of those extreme couponers, only for teenagers.

He'll do anything for a buck. Maybe even give up his seat on the plane.

I walk over to him.

"Oh, hey, Bruno," I say, even though we're not friends. We're not even acquaintances. In fact, my only interaction with Bruno has been one time sophomore year when we were assigned to debate each other in world history. It was kind of awful, because Bruno is so crazy that he just kept coming up with all these arguments that had no bearing on what we were even talking about. It was like playing a game with someone who didn't know the rules—he just kept saying crazy things, and I had no idea how to respond. I still got an A, though—I think our teacher was impressed by how I handled everything Bruno was throwing at me.

"Hey, Amanda," he says, not looking up from his phone.

"I'm just wondering where you're sitting on the plane," I say, deciding not to correct him about my name. The last thing I want to do is start this off on a bad note. If I'm going to ask him to do me a favor, I don't want to be contentious with the guy.

"If you're worried about my ringworm, you don't have to be," he says, with the world-weary tone of someone who's been through a lot and doesn't feel the need to pander to people who know nothing about his life. "It's not contagious unless you come into direct contact with it."

"Oh, no," I say. "I'm not . . . I mean, I'm not worried about getting ringworm from you."

"Well you should be," he says, glancing up at me and then back down to his phone. "It's highly contagious."

Ooookay. "I just wanted to see if maybe you'd switch seats with me."

"No."

"Why not?"

"Because I like my seat."

"But I have a window seat," I say.

"I hate window seats."

"I'll pay you twenty bucks."

This is enough to get him interested, and he looks up from his phone. "Why?"

"Why?"

"Yeah, why do you want to switch seats with me so bad?"

"I just need a different seat," I say firmly. I'm desperate, but not desperate enough to tell Bruno all my personal business. Although if I'm being completely honest, maybe I am. When faced with a choice between having to tell Bruno that I'm having issues with Liam and Izzy and actually having to sit with Liam and Izzy, I think maybe I'd rather just tell Bruno.

"You slept with someone and now you have to get away from them," Bruno says.

"No!"

"It's about a guy," he says.

"Sort of," I say. "See, my friend—"

"No." He holds his hand up, shushing me. "I don't want to know." He pulls on his bottom lip, considering. "Fifty bucks."

"Fifty bucks?" I repeat, incredulous.

"Well, yeah," he says. "You're obviously having some

kind of personal problem, and you must be pretty desperate to come over here and ask me, a person you don't even know, if I'll switch seats with you on the plane. Not to mention you offered to pay me for it. So I'm assuming if you're willing to do all that, then you're probably willing to pay more than twenty bucks."

I open my mouth to protest, but I don't know if it's the best idea to get into some kind of back-and-forth with him. And in the grand scheme of things, is thirty extra dollars that much to haggle about?

"Sold."

It's the best fifty dollars I ever spent.

Bruno's seat is all the way in the back of the plane, which I think I read somewhere is actually the worst place you can be if there's ever a crash. But whatever. There's way more of a chance that I'm going to end up in a fight with Liam and Izzy than there is of this plane crashing. According to Google, the plane has a one-in-eleven-million chance of crashing. The chances of me getting into some kind of drama with Liam and Izzy are probably like one in two.

And the fact that the seat is all the way in the back of the plane is perfect. I won't have to see anyone. Of course, I have no idea who I'm going to be sitting with. Probably one of Bruno's crazy friends. But who cares. I'll just slip in my earbuds and not listen to a thing that person has to say.

I'd much rather put up with some clown sitting next to me than have to—

"Excuse me," someone says. "But I need to get to my seat, and you're blocking the aisle."

I look up.

Liam.

"What are you doing?" I blurt.

"That's my seat," he says, indicating the one next to me. "And you're blocking it."

"It is not your seat," I say.

"Then whose seat is it?"

"It's . . ." Damn it. I should have asked Bruno who he was sitting next to. Not that it really matters. "Someone else's," I finish lamely.

"We need to talk," Liam says, sitting down next to me, apparently not concerned that he's taking someone else's seat.

"We can't," I say firmly. "Pretty soon whoever's supposed to be sitting there is going to come along and kick you out of that seat."

"No, they're not," he says easily. "Because I switched seats."

"You switched seats with who?"

"Jack Busey," he says. "He was sitting next to Bruno."

"But why would you do that?" I ask, panicked. I stand

up and look to the front of the plane, where, sure enough, Bruno and Jack are sitting up near Izzy, who has a huge scowl on her face.

"Because I saw you talking to Bruno," Liam says, and his voice goes from defiant to soft. "And I wanted to sit next to you."

I sit back down, sliding over to the empty window seat, and turn away from him. The sun is shining, but I know in just a few hours I'm going to be in the dreariness of the New England weather. It's almost comforting, in a way. I'm not sad to be leaving Florida. I'm happy to be going home, back to the comfort of my bed and the comfort of home. I'm sick of the sun, I'm sick of possibility. I just want to get home and wallow in my misery.

"So is it okay if I sit here?" he asks.

I don't trust myself to talk, so instead, I just nod.

He looks at me, his eyes so bright and blue, the eyes of the only boy I've ever loved. I want so desperately for him to love me back, but it just didn't work out that way. He doesn't love me. He never did.

"I don't . . . Liam, I want to talk to you, I do." The words are out of my mouth before I even know that I mean them. But it's true. I do want to talk to Liam. Part of me knows that it will be extremely hard—staying in his life, being his friend when he knows how I feel about him and doesn't return my feelings. But it might be harder to let him go completely. He's my best friend.

"Good." He nods. "Aven—"

I hold my hand up, slightly annoyed that he thinks he can just decide he wants to talk to me now, in this moment, when the other night he told me he needed time, like I was just supposed to wait around until he was ready. "But not right now. I need some time to process how I feel about all this. I need some time to figure out how this new friendship of ours is going to look." I turn toward the window again, this time because I don't want him to see the pain on my face. The last thing I want is for Liam to feel sorry for me.

"Aven, I don't want to be friends with you anymore."

My breath catches in my chest. He doesn't want to be friends anymore? That's what he came over here to tell me? I can't even look at him. His every word is a dagger straight to my heart, tearing it apart one tiny rip at a time, destroying me.

"Please," I say. "Please, Liam, just leave me alone." A tear slides down my cheek, hot and salty, before I can stop it. It hits my lips, and I don't bother to brush it away.

"Aven, look at me." Liam takes my chin in his hand, pulling it toward him gently, forcing me to look at him. His touch is soft and his eyes are so warm and kind, I can't help thinking that maybe there's been some kind of terrible mistake, that maybe he's decided he does want to be friends with me after all. Who decides they don't want to be friends with you and then looks at you the way he's looking at me now, with so much kindness?

"I want to try this," he says. He takes a deep breath. "I've always been afraid of the risk, but I want to try it."

"You want to try being friends?" I ask, frowning. What is he talking about, afraid of the risk? The risk of what? The risk of breaking my heart? Well, if he's worried about that, he can stop. My heart's already been broken.

"No, I want to try, um, this. You know, being together."

My heart starts thumping and my stomach is somer-saulting and my skin is tingling. He's looking at me with that same kind look in his eyes, and I want so badly to tell him yes, to throw myself into his arms, to try and make everything I've ever wanted and hoped for us come true.

But of all the times I've played this moment in my head, over and over and over again for years, it's never been Liam sitting next to me telling me he wants to *try*. It's Liam telling me he feels the same way, that he wants to be with me, that he thinks we'd be perfect together. I don't want to be with someone who's not sure. Especially not Liam. Because with him, I've never been so sure about anything in my life.

I shake my head. "No," I say. "It's not good enough."

"What's not?"

"It's not good enough. You have to be sure. You can't just want to try, Liam." I'm looking at his face, hoping that maybe I've missed something, that maybe he really does want this just as badly as I do. But I can see the doubt on his face.

"Liam," I say, before he can say anything else. "Please, if you've ever cared about me, please . . . can you just leave me alone? Just for a little while."

He goes to open his mouth to say something, but I repeat, "*Please*," and after a second, he gets up and leaves.

A minute later, Jack Busey slides into the seat next to me.

I turn to the window so he can't see me cry.

TWELVE

I THOUGHT THE FLIGHT WOULD LEAVE ME A sopping, crying mess and feel never-ending, but it's actually kind of the opposite. In fact, after a few tears, there's actually no crying. There's just this weird emptiness in my body, an ache that feels like nothing I've ever felt before. It's like my soul is grieving or something. I know that sounds over the top and dramatic, but it's true. So much of my energy and hoping had gone into Liam, and this trip, that now that it's over, I just feel . . . empty.

I'm in a fog as I walk up to baggage claim. I watch the bags as they all come spinning by, scanning them for my turquoise suitcase. I thought I was being so clever by not bringing the standard black bag, but most of my classmates must have had the same idea, because they all have bags in an array of colors. I'm just about to reach for my suitcase when someone grabs it off the carousel and sets it down in front of me.

Liam.

Again.

"Liam," I say, sighing. "You're not listening to me, and I really need you to. I said—"

"No," he says firmly, shaking his head. "*You* need to listen to *me*."

"Excuse me?" I say, annoyed.

"Yeah," he says. "You need to listen to me. Because I obviously didn't do a very good job of letting you know how I feel." He stands my suitcase up and looks at me. "When I said I wanted to try this, I was serious. I did mean I wanted to try it, but not the way you thought. I meant that I'm afraid."

I frown. "Why would you be afraid?"

"Because," he says. He reaches out and takes my hand, and it's different from the way he took it on the plane. This time, his grip is firm, like there's an intention behind it. "I was afraid of losing you."

"But why would you lose me?" I ask.

"If this doesn't work out . . ." He shakes his head. "I don't know what I would do. I think I've been lying to myself this whole time, telling myself we were just friends, when deep down, I was just afraid of getting hurt."

The tears come to my eyes, but this time, they're tears of happiness.

"You have to be sure," I say, almost scared to let myself believe it. "You have to be really sure. You can't just think you feel this way, and then in a couple weeks decide it's not right." I look at him, at the kindness and warmth in his eyes, the way he's looking at me like I'm all he can see, even though we're surrounded by people.

"I'm sure," he says firmly. He pulls me close to him, and I'm in his arms and it's wonderful and perfect and better than I ever could have imagined. "Every second since you told me how you felt, I couldn't stop thinking about you. And just now, when you told me to leave you alone on the plane, Aven, I missed you. I was on the same plane as you and it had only been a few minutes and I was already missing you." He shakes his head. "I'm sorry it took me so long to admit to myself how I felt. I'm sorry I was too scared. But I'm not anymore." He shakes his head. "It's you, Aven. It's always been you."

A tear slips down my cheek, and he pushes it away with the pad of his thumb. "Don't cry," he says.

"I'm crying because I'm happy," I say.

He smiles, that same smile I fell in love with all those years ago. Only now it's the smile of the boy who likes me back. He kisses me then, his lips soft and sure and perfect.

Then we just stand there for a few moments, our foreheads pushed together, grinning at each other like two idiots.

When we pull apart, I take a deep breath. "Izzy . . . ," I start.

He nods, his face serious. "We'll talk to her together."

"Okay."

"Come on," he says, taking my hand. "Let's go home."

The whole bus ride back to school, Liam and I stare at each other giddily. It's weird—I always thought that if we ever did get together, there'd be an adjustment period. That it would be weird and awkward for a little while, but the reality is just that it doesn't feel strange at all. The only thing it feels is *right*.

But as soon as we get off the bus, Izzy is standing there, waiting for us.

"Hi," I say, dropping Liam's hand. I don't want to rub it into her face that we're together now. Liam instinctively goes to grab my hand again, but I give him a look, and he nods in understanding.

"Izzy," I say. "We can—"

But she holds up her hand. "I'm not upset."

"You're not?" Liam asks.

"I am, but I'm not." She takes in a deep breath. "It wasn't working out with us. And I just . . . I don't want to make a big thing about it." She bites her lip, and I can tell she's trying hard not to cry.

"Just so you know," I say, "nothing happened when you two were together."

She smiles. "I know," she says. "I know you wouldn't do something like that."

"I'd like to still be friends," Liam says.

I nod, because I want to be friends with Izzy, too. Of course, another part of me knows just how weird that's going to be. The three of us being friends, with the roles reversed—me as Liam's girlfriend, Izzy as our friend.

But Izzy shakes her head. "I do, too," she says. "But maybe . . . maybe not right now."

She leans into me then, her silky blond hair brushing against my face. "It's always been you," she whispers into my ear. "I always knew that." She straightens back up. "Take care of each other," she says, and then, before we can reply, she's moving her way down the sidewalk toward the parking lot, her hair swishing behind her.

Liam looks at me. "You okay?"

"Yeah," I say as he pulls me close. "I just wish we didn't have to hurt her."

"Me too." He strokes my hair, his touch soft and comforting. I close my eyes for a moment, savoring this feeling of happiness.

There's just one little niggling thing bothering me—Lyla and Quinn. Now that Liam and I are together, I want to tell them. In fact, they're the only ones I want to tell. And it's not just because I want them to be happy for me, although of course that's part of it. I want to talk to them, to share with them. I miss them. Besides Liam, they're the only real best friends I've ever had.

But what else can I really do? I already finagled things so that we were all in the same room for a whole weekend. We even hung out for a day and nothing changed.

And then I have an idea. A crazy, insane, brilliant idea.

Liam and I grab our bags, and the idea is still percolating in my brain, turning around and around like a rock in a tumbler, forming into something that might just work.

"So maybe you can come over later?" Liam asks. "Unless you just want to come with me now? My mom's waiting in the traffic circle." He tilts his head toward his mom's car, which is still pretty far back in the line, but inching closer.

"Nah, that's okay," I say. "I'll just text you later." I take in a deep breath. "I think . . . I think I'm going to try to talk to Quinn and Lyla."

Liam's eyes flash with surprise. And then he nods. "I think you should."

"You do?"

"Yeah. I mean, look what happened when you finally talked to me." He grins, then leans down and kisses me. My stomach explodes with butterflies. Will I ever get used to this? Him, kissing me? It's the scariest, most wonderful, craziest feeling I've ever had.

He squeezes my hand, then kisses me one more time. "I'll call you later," he says before disappearing into the throng of kids all heading for their parents' cars.

I watch him go, my heart filled with so much love for him. I give myself another second to enjoy this new reality, this new amazing, terrifying, thrilling reality.

And then I turn around and head toward the school, ready to put my crazy plan into action.

I was supposed to text my parents when the bus pulled in, so they'd know when to leave to come and get me. But I don't. Instead, I text them and tell them the bus is running a little late, and that I'll let them know as soon as we get in.

Then I take a deep breath and text Lyla and Quinn, and tell them that I'm locked in the bathroom by the gym, and that I need help.

I know. It's stupid—how the hell would I get locked in the bathroom by the gym? I mean, if I needed to use the bathroom, that's the last bathroom I would ever use, since it's nowhere near the front of the school. It's a totally unbelievable lie, and there's a good chance the two of them won't believe it.

But the thing about the bathroom by the gym is that I have a key to it. It's the bathroom closest to where the Student Action Committee meets, and one time our faculty adviser gave me the key and then forgot to ask for it back. It's been sitting on my key chain for, like, ever. I haven't been keeping it intentionally or anything, I just always seem to forget to turn it in.

A few minutes later, I'm out of sight around the corner of the hallway, waiting for Lyla and Quinn, crossing my fingers and holding my breath that they're actually going to show. But when a couple of more minutes pass by, I'm starting to think they're not going to come—that maybe they either don't care, or that they saw through my whole "I'm locked in the bathroom" ploy. But then I hear the sound of someone's suitcase being wheeled down the corridor, followed by voices.

The bathroom door opens and shuts, and I wait a few seconds, trying to time it correctly. I need to make sure that they're far enough into the bathroom so they can't escape, but they can't be in there *too* long, because once it becomes clear I'm not really there, they're probably going to leave.

I count to thirty slowly in my head, figuring thirty seconds should be just enough time.

When I walk into the bathroom, the two of them have just finished looking through the stalls.

"Aven!" Quinn exclaims. "Why the hell did you tell us you were locked in the bathroom?"

"Yeah," Lyla says, sounding annoyed.

I don't say anything. Instead, I just turn around and lock the door behind me. "What the hell are you *doing*?" Quinn asks.

I slip the key into my pocket. I wonder briefly if maybe they're going to do something crazy like try to take the key from me. You know, like, forcefully. But those two wouldn't try to get physical with me. At least, I don't think they would.

"I'm sick of this," I say. "I'm sick of not being friends. I'm ready to make up." I take a deep breath. "And none of us are leaving this bathroom until we do."

THIRTEEN

THERE'S A BEAT OF SILENCE AFTER I MAKE
this declaration, like they can't believe I would be so crazy
as to do something like lock them in a bathroom, like it's so
insane and incomprehensible that there's no way it can actually be happening.

Then it hits them.

"*What?*" Quinn exclaims. "Aven, you've lost it." She
moves toward the door and tries the handle, even though
she's just seen me lock it. She holds her hand out. "Give it."

"Give it?" I repeat.

"Yeah. Give me the key."

I shake my head. "No."

"No?" She turns around and looks to Lyla for help.
But there's no way I'm letting the two of them gang up on
me and turn this into an "ohmygod, isn't Aven so crazy"
moment.

"No." I shake my head. "We need to talk."

Lyla sighs and rolls her suitcase over to the other side of the bathroom. She leans against the window ledge. "We already talked, Aven," she says. "We talked all day yesterday."

"Really talk," I say. "About our fight. About what happened."

"No way," Quinn says. "No. I'm happy. I don't want to start getting into all kinds of old shit." She crosses her arms over her chest, like the conversation is done just because she's decided it is.

"You're happy?" I ask. "Since when?"

"Yeah," Lyla says. "I thought you said you were so upset yesterday?"

Quinn starts to open her mouth to explain, but then shuts it. "No," she says firmly. "This is not any of your business. I think it's great that we were able to spend some time together yesterday without wanting to kill each other. But our friendship is over. It's time to move on."

I feel the tears starting to form behind my eyes again, the crushing sense of disappointment that flows through me. But maybe Quinn is right. Maybe some friendships just aren't supposed to last forever. Maybe some friendships run their course, or end for reasons that aren't anyone's fault.

I'm about to think that maybe I should unlock the door and let everyone out of here when Lyla mutters, "Easy for you to say."

"What's that supposed to mean?" Quinn asks.

"I just mean that it's probably easy for you to move on, since you're not the one who got hurt."

"Are you kidding?" Quinn asks. "Of course I got hurt."

Yes! They're talking! This might be working! "We all got hurt," I say, in an effort to insert myself into the conversation.

"Yeah, you got hurt, but it was your own fault," Lyla says. "You got hurt because you told my secret."

"I was never told it was a secret," Quinn says, turning to look at me. Lyla looks at me, too, the two of them staring at me, like I hold the key about who's to blame.

"I don't remember if you specifically told me not to tell anyone," I say to Lyla honestly. "And even if you had, I probably would have told Quinn anyway, because I can't imagine you would have meant not to tell her."

"I didn't mean not to tell her," Lyla says. "But you did, and then Quinn told her mom, so you're both to blame."

"That doesn't make any sense," I say. "Why is what Quinn did my fault?"

"Oh, thanks a lot," Quinn says, shooting me a dirty look. She takes a deep breath. "Look, can we not do this? Seriously, it's stupid."

"It's not stupid," I say. "I miss you guys." My voice is cracking on this last part, and it's all I can do to not start crying.

Quinn and Lyla look at each other awkwardly, and I realize I've never told them this. At least, not recently. I've told them that we need to talk about what happened, that we need to process our feelings and blah blah blah. But I've never actually just come out and said how I feel.

Maybe that email—the one that told me I needed to tell the truth—was as much about my friendship with Quinn and Lyla as it was about Liam. And telling the truth to Liam was painful and messy and hurt like hell, but the payoff was more amazing than I ever could have imagined.

"I just really miss you guys," I say again. "You guys were like my sisters, like my family. I haven't had friends like you since then, and I'm not sure I'm going to ever again." I shake my head. "And I'm not sure, but maybe . . . maybe because we hadn't ever hurt each other before, our fight felt worse than it actually was."

"No," Lyla says, shaking her head. "It was really that bad." Her voice cracks. "At least, it was for me."

"No," I say slowly, making sure to choose my words carefully. "You're misunderstanding me. What I meant was it felt worse because we didn't expect it. We thought we were the only people in each other's lives who we'd never get hurt by, even unintentionally. So when it happened, it felt like a double betrayal."

Lyla nods. She starts to cry, tears streaming down her face. "I just felt like you guys didn't care about me at all, like you just told my secret and didn't understand why I felt the way I did. You guys acted like I was being stupid."

Quinn reaches over and takes a paper towel out of the dispenser and hands it to Lyla. Then she walks over to her and puts her hand on her shoulder. I walk over and take Lyla's other shoulder, and we stand there and just let her cry for a while. Because the thing is, as much as Quinn and I were hurt by all of this, this is mostly about Lyla. She's the one who was hurt the most.

"I never wanted to hurt you," I say. "I'm so, so sorry, Lyla. You have to know that if I knew what was going to happen, I never would have told Quinn."

"And I never would have told my mom," Quinn says.

"I know," Lyla says. "I know you wouldn't have." She blots her eyes with the paper towel, smudging it with her mascara.

"Then why were you so mad?" I ask quietly. "If you knew we didn't do it on purpose?"

She thinks about it. "I guess I was just so angry," she says. "I was so angry at my parents for putting me in that weird position, of making me choose between them." She shakes her head. "And I just felt like I was bottling everything inside, and it just . . . it wasn't fair, but it needed a place to go. And so I put it on you two."

We all fall silent for a moment, considering. "Are you guys mad at me?" Lyla asks.

"No!" I say quickly. "I'm not mad at you, Lyla. That's totally understandable."

"I just wish you would have talked to us about it instead of shutting us out," Quinn says. "We were your best friends. I wanted to talk to you so bad, I wanted to make sure you were okay." Her voice is filled with emotion, remembering. "Every time I'd see you in the halls at school I'd get so sad, missing you, thinking about you going through everything alone."

"I know," Lyla says. "I wish I would have talked to you guys. I'm starting to think I have a problem with facing things head on. It's like I have to just keep moving forward, pretending I'm right even when I know I'm not. It's like what happened with Derrick."

"What happened with Derrick?" I ask curiously.

"We broke up."

"How come?" Quinn asks.

"It wasn't working," Lyla says. "And I couldn't . . . I couldn't see it. And I just kept going with it, trying to pretend everything was fine, when it wasn't. And I think I did the same with you guys. I had shut you out, and it was more important for me to convince myself I was right so I wouldn't have to deal with my feelings around it." She shakes her head and wipes her eyes again, then tosses the paper towel into the trash can. "I'm sorry," she says. "I feel like I'm not making any sense."

"No, it makes perfect sense," Quinn says. "It's like you make a decision, you go on a path, and then it's just easier to keep going on that path instead of actually dealing with anything real. I was doing the same thing."

"You were?" Lyla asks curiously. "With what?"

"Stanford," Quinn says. "I thought it was all I wanted, and now . . . well, now I don't."

"Wow," I say, kind of shocked. As long as I've known her, Quinn has wanted to go to Stanford. For her to say she's not sure about that, well . . . it must have been some journey to get there.

"Yeah," Quinn says softly. She takes in a deep breath. "So what about you?" she asks me. "Have you ever kept doing something that you knew was wrong, just because it was easier?"

"Liam," I say automatically. "I never told him how I felt, and this whole time I just kept being friends with him." I feel my cheeks redden as I think about earlier, kissing him, his hands in my hair, his lips on mine. "Until this weekend."

"Ohmygod," Lyla says, turning to me. "You told Liam you liked him?"

I nod.

"And?" Quinn prompts.

"And we're kind of together now."

They two of them squeal and hug me, and for a second, it feels like old times.

"Did you tell him because of your email?" Quinn asks as she pulls away.

"Yes." I nod.

"My email's the reason I don't want to go to Stanford anymore," Quinn admits.

"My email's the reason I broke up with Derrick," Lyla says. "And why I'm kind of hooking up with Beckett Cross."

We all stare at each other.

"So we all did what our emails told us," I say.

Three nods.

"So even though we hadn't even spoken in years, major things in our lives happened because of each other," I say excitedly. "Don't you guys see? It's like our connection can't be broken."

Quinn looks at me skeptically. "Please don't tell me you actually believe that," she says, like she thinks it's akin to me admitting I still believe in Santa Claus. Again, she looks to Lyla again for help, but Lyla just shrugs.

"Don't look at me," Lyla says. "It's as good of an explanation as any."

I smile at her, and Quinn's face softens. "Ah, what the hell," she says. "Our connection was strong."

"Don't you see?" I say. "It's a sign we have to be friends again."

"I don't know," Lyla says. "So much has happened."

"But if we don't try," Quinn says slowly, thinking about

it, "then aren't we doing just what we said we didn't want to do anymore? Keeping things the same because we're afraid to be crazy, or trust, or tell the truth?"

It takes me a second to realize she's mentioned the three things we agreed to do in the emails we sent all those years ago. She remembered. And she's right.

"She's right," I say, turning to Lyla.

"I know," Lyla says, and her tears are back, making her eyes shiny again. "I know she is. And I just . . . I miss you guys so much. And I'm so sorry."

We all start crying then, and our arms are around each other, and it feels like everything's different but also the same.

"So can we try to be friends again?" I ask.

"Yes," Lyla says.

"Yes," Quinn says.

"It won't be easy," I warn them. "We're going to have to talk more, and we're all going to be going to college soon. . . ."

"We can get through it," Lyla says. "My new promise to myself is to try to be happy. And you guys make me happy."

"That's what you wrote on your paper?" I ask, shocked. "The new ones we wrote yesterday? That you wanted to be happy?"

Lyla nods.

"That's what I wrote, too," I say.

"Me too," Quinn says.

I squeal and do a little jump. "See?" I say. "The three of us are connected! Just like I said."

Quinn shakes her head, but she's laughing. "If I agree with that, will you let us out of this bathroom?" She wrinkles her nose. "It smells like old gym socks."

"Only if you guys agree to come over to my house after school tomorrow," I say. "We can catch up and I'll make my mom whip up a plate of her nachos."

"Ooh," Lyla says, moaning in pleasure. "I almost forgot about your mom's nachos."

"And can we have those chocolate shakes she makes?" Quinn asks. "The ones with the double fudge ice cream?"

"Of course," I say, heading over to unlock the door.

I hold it open for them, and the three of us pass through it and out into the hallway.

I know it's not going to be easy. There's a lot of water under the bridge, and I'm not the same girl I was two years ago. Hell, I'm not the same girl I was two *days* ago. And neither are Lyla and Quinn.

But maybe that's what makes friendships so important. They help you grow and change and give you someone to lean on while you're doing that. At least, the good ones do. It just took us a little while to figure that out.

I push myself in between Quinn and Lyla, linking my arms through each of theirs. It's the way we used to walk down the halls in junior high, just to annoy people.

"Oh God," Quinn says, rolling her eyes. But there's a smile on her face.

"Ready?" I ask.

"Yup," Lyla replies, and the three of us start walking toward the front door. We're ready. Ready for the future, ready for each other, ready for the promise of happiness.